Wolf Wing

THE CLAIDI JOURNALS ✠ BOOK IV

Wolf Wing

Tanith Lee

DUTTON CHILDREN'S BOOKS ✠ NEW YORK

NEW HANOVER COUNTY PUBLIC LIBRARY
201 Chestnut Street
Wilmington, NC 28401

This book is a work of fiction. Names, characters, places, and incidents are either the product of the author's imagination or are used fictitiously, and any resemblance to actual persons, living or dead, business establishments, events, or locales is entirely coincidental. Some phrases and references have been changed in this edition for the convenience of American readers.

Copyright © 2002 by Tanith Lee

All rights reserved.
No part of this publication may be reproduced or transmitted in any form or by any means, electronic or mechanical, including photocopy, recording, or any information storage and retrieval system now known or to be invented, without permission in writing from the publisher, except by a reviewer who wishes to quote brief passages in connection with a review written for inclusion in a magazine, newspaper, or broadcast.

Library of Congress Cataloging-in-Publication Data
Lee, Tanith.
Wolf Wing / by Tanith Lee.—1st American ed.
p. cm.—(The Claidi journals; bk. 4)
Summary: Following their marriage, Claidi and Argul are drawn back to her birthplace, the House, where yet again they are led to seek the answer to the riddle of Ustareth.
ISBN 0-525-47162-6
[1. Fantasy.] I. Title.
PZ7.L5149 Wr 2003
[Fic]—dc21   2003040853

Published in the United States 2003 by Dutton Children's Books, a division of Penguin Young Readers Group
345 Hudson Street, New York, New York 10014
www.penguin.com

Originally published in Great Britain 2002
by Hodder Children's Books, London

Typography by Gloria Cheng
Printed in USA • First American Edition
2 4 6 8 10 9 7 5 3 1

YOUTH IS *NOT* WASTED ON THE YOUNG.
Fact

TOWER FAMILY TREES

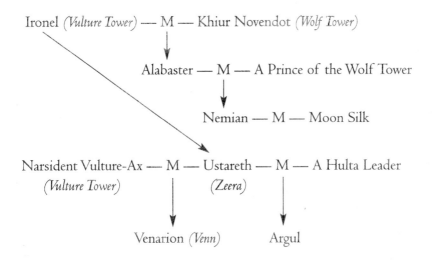

Ironel *(Vulture Tower)* — M — Khiur Novendot *(Wolf Tower)*

Alabaster — M — A Prince of the Wolf Tower

Nemian — M — Moon Silk

Narsident Vulture-Ax — M — Ustareth — M — A Hulta Leader
(Vulture Tower)   *(Zeera)*

Venarion *(Venn)*   Argul

Jizania Tiger *(Tiger Tower)* — M — Wasliwa Star *(The House)*

Twilight Star — M — Fengrey Raven
                 (Raven Tower)

Winter Raven *(originally called Claidis)*

M = *who married whom*
——➤ = *what children were then born*

CONTENTS

Wolf Wing

BOOKMARKS

It isn't that we're unhappy.

We are happy. We're together.

Only nothing is ever straightforward, is it. Do you find that? There's always some complication, some extra *something*.

And what seems about to be just a happy golden flight through the bluest air—

Well, it's as if a cloud keeps covering up the sun.

I suppose it's habit now, turning back to my "diary-journal"— this book. Will I always do this, make these wiggly black marks over the whitish paper, these marks which are letters and words—but which are really feelings, thoughts, confessions—

Maybe I always will.

✦ ✦ ✦

We'd been standing at one of Yinyay's windows, Argul and I, as we traveled through the air, always southward, toward Peshamba.

I said, "You do know Yinyay can almost certainly locate the Hulta? She found them before. Do you think—?"

And Argul didn't say anything.

Then he said what he'd said before: "A leader can't really go back to being a leader, Claidi. I'm not sure he can even go *back*. I might not be welcome."

"Oh, but Argul—they're your *family*—"

"Yes," he said. "I know that."

"Perhaps if you just tried? I mean, Blurn—"

"Blurn took over from me when I left, and is now leader. Despite anything he might have said, Claidi, despite being a good mate, he'll have changed. You do, if you're leader. You have to." He went on staring down Yinyay's whirling-along length. She wasn't really whirling then, but just going fast and smooth. The landscape below seemed to be grasslands, or else a green desert. The sky was morning-bright. "Really," Argul said softly.

And after that, nothing else.

So I left it.

He had given it all up, his leadership, the Hulta family, and his lifelong friends, in order to find and rescue me, in order to make sure I survived the plots of the Wolf Tower and the Raven Tower.

Of course, I thought, he *must* miss the Hulta. Even I did, and I hadn't been with them that long. Argul was *born* Hulta.

For nineteen years he'd lived with them, almost four of those as their king.

Although it wasn't my fault, exactly, I couldn't help thinking it was because of me he'd lost all that, and apparently *really* lost it all, for good. He seemed to think he was exiled.

That evening Yinyay landed and parked on a hilltop.

Argul and I flew out of a top window and dived and played about in the sky. We watched the sun set over some hills, then flew up even higher to watch it sink again.

I say *flew*, but naturally we weren't flying as such, as you know, but more like walking or running in the sky.

It is wonderful, doing this. Exhilarating—and the tingle of amazement never quite goes away, or at least not for me.

I veered and swerved up to the lowest clouds, touched their fleecy smoke, rushed down again to the richer, more breathable air, gasping and laughing. I thought over and over, How am I DOING this? Even though I know I'm doing it because of the diamond Power ring that was Ustareth's. Just as Argul can "fly" because of the sapphire on the charm, which hangs around his neck.

After the flight, we landed in a valley, and for exercise walked on the ground back up to Yinyay's white Tower, gleaming in the afterglow.

"I miss Sirree," I said, not thinking. "She was the best horse. I miss riding."

"Right. I do, too."

"And the dogs and monkeys—"

He didn't speak, like before.

I thought, *Am I going to have to be careful now, never to say anything*

[5]

that makes him think of the Hulta? He had seemed almost unnaturally at home with all the science-magic. With Yinyay, all of it. Now I wondered if it *had* been unnatural—that is, if he'd been pretending, to me, or to himself.

I said, "I didn't mean to remind you," and Argul said flatly, "I'm reminded all the time, Claidi. I don't *want* to forget the Hulta, do I?"

Later, after dinner had laid itself on a silvery table high up in the all-window room near Yinyay's top, Argul casually remarked, "What a lazy life. It's too easy, all this."

I pictured how the Hulta would have made camp, and the one big campfire, and the little fires all about. The lighting of the lamps, the cooking of food. I thought of the Hulta gathering around the fires, and the king and his men having a meeting—Argul, Blurn, Mehm, Ro—shining in the firelight. The horses moving lightly at their pickets, the dogs walking about, glossy and calm. Bits of music, laughter, jingling of horse bells and earrings. Evening stars overhead, and open sky. And things to do in the morning.

Argul and I talked about something else while we ate the dinner, which was delicious as usual, in Yinyay's Tower.

Soon I forgot about the strange feeling that had come over and between us. It was gone.

Until of course, it came back.

Missing things . . .

Stupidly perhaps, *I* missed talking to Yinyay herself. I'd had quite a few chats with her on Ustareth's Star-ship, when I first came back from the Rise. Yin had been a dolly-snake then, elegantly balanced on her tail, gently handing me cups of tea held by the tendrils of her hair.

Now she was the huge Tower. From the outside, you saw her turn her face, stories up, far above, looking mildly around, a beautiful watcher, guarding us, perhaps scanning the weather or the stars. If you called up to her, the face would look down. She would smile her quiet, angelic smile. She was and is a machine, but she had been also a companion. Now that she's all around us, she's much further away.

Yinyay had become—well, like a god. Sort of. Powerful, kind, always just about to be seen in the distance, yet unreachable.

Oh, I don't mean she doesn't do *everything* for us we ask. She does. But—it's the gadgets and mechanisms of her Tower itself which do these things.

Though we named the Tower "Yinyay," it's a bit hard to remember it's actually *her*.

Anyway, journeying in Yinyay all the long way from the north to the south, not always going very fast, and often parking in some pleasant spot for a while, took us one whole month, or "moonth" (as Chylomba had called them).

We were going to be married at Peshamba.

I had no intention of writing in this book anything about that. I was superstitious, because *look* what had happened the first time we were supposed to get married!!! (And, for that matter, the second.)

This was going to be so different, too.

It wouldn't be a Hulta wedding.

No one we knew would be there.

The customs wouldn't be the same, either.

And I had sold my wedding dress. A goat had gotten married in it instead.

I remembered Peshamba so vividly: the fields of flowers as you got near, the turquoise lake, and the glamorous town with its jewelry towers and windows.

This was where I had first really *seen* Argul—that astonishing night of the festival, the dance, the peacock in the moonlit garden—magical Peshamba.

But when we came to Peshamba, it wasn't as I remembered at all.

The north had been full of snow. Well, the place was actually called Winter, after all. But there was a kind of winter now, in Peshamba.

I recalled how last time we were here, it had been snow which interrupted Argul and me in the peacock garden, before we could get anything said or properly sorted out. (After which Nemian had appeared and *really* ruined our chances.)

Snow in Peshamba, however, had been pretty. The town had still looked like a charming toy.

I thought it must have snowed recently now. Then the snow had melted. But it had taken all the flowers, and the leaves off the trees. And the color from the sky and lake. And somehow from a lot of the buildings.

A bleak, hard, glassy sky hung high overhead. And even

from the distant place where Yin had landed, you could see the smoke fumes rising from Peshamba's chimneys, and curdling there blackly in the still, white air, so the whole town was under a cloud.

Argul had suggested that we not come zooming down in Yinyay. It could cause a commotion and might set off Peshamba's defenses, which were mechanical and quite famously dangerous.

So after Yinyay had brought us down to earth well clear of the town, she reduced herself for the first time since we met her again in the north.

The original plan was for her to stay doll-size, since Peshambans are used to (average-sized) mechanical dolls. But when Yinyay had done this, she herself said if we didn't need her just then, she would prefer to make herself very tiny. In this way, she explained, she could "be at one" with all her own mechanisms and new abilities to do with becoming a flying Tower. (She seemed to find this prospect exciting.)

Neither Argul nor I objected. (Was he perhaps glad? The lazy life—gone.)

Yinyay then shrank in a sudden alarming rush that made me blink. One moment she was there, about my height, and then she had sort of *snapped* away.

"Where—*is* she?" I gawped.

"I have her," said Argul. And he showed me the shrunk Yinyay, who must have darted somehow into his hand, a little teeny pearly speck, like a pin's head, lying there on his dark palm. I now couldn't see any of her features, even her tail.

It seemed she'd previously given Argul a carrying pouch for this situation. He put her into it and asked if I wanted to carry the pouch, or should he.

I felt totally bemused. "Oh, you can have her—" I vaguely muttered. Because it had seemed suddenly untrusting to say, "Give her to me."

Of course, we can call her back to any size any time we want to. I felt tempted to try it at once. Somehow her going like that left me feeling as if there were a huge hole in everything where she'd been.

So anyway, we went on foot through the cold-scorched grasses, and came to the cold pale lake, and walked over the bridge into Peshamba, through an apparently unguarded gate, under high windows reflecting the blank sky.

THE CLOCKWORK
WEDDING

We didn't stay at the Travelers' Rest, where we did before, with the Hulta. Instead we took a big room in a house that rented big rooms. The building had rose-red walls that the Peshamban winter had faded to a dull, rusty pink. There was a large garden outside, with grapevines that had gone black and lots of bare trees and flowerbeds with headless flower stalks standing up in them.

"It must have been a bad snow," I said to the woman who showed us to the room.

"Not a snow. Leaves and blooms survive *under* snow," she said. "A cruel frost."

That evening the frost resettled, as apparently it had been doing for ages. The air sparked with chill and the stars flashed wildly like insane, bright eyes. In the morning, all the roofs would again be thick with white frost-scales.

Downstairs, where we had dinner at the house-table with the house-family in their colored silks, and several other travelers, the weather was discussed.

"I say it's been upset," said a man who wore his fur cloak to the table.

"Yes, it's certainly not right."

"Twenty solid nights of frost. Never happened here in living memory."

This was all from the visitors. (They seemed to know more about Peshamba than the Peshambans, who just sat there politely, neither arguing nor agreeing.)

Fur Cloak's girlfriend, who had on a fur coat, chipped in, "Well, *I* say it's witchcraft. I say someone's cast a jealous eye on Peshamba." There was a real silence at this. Everyone, I think, put down their knives or forks and looked at her. Not put out, the FCG tossed her straw-yellow hair and added, "Everyone knows Peshamba is a prize no one can take; it's too well defended by its machines and fighter-dolls. So someone's taken a spite against it."

Fur Cloak cleared his throat. The FCG shrugged and drank her tea.

Then the fat, good-looking visitor, who said he sold elephants (he'd tried to sell us one), announced, "*I* heard someone's tugged all the warm weather off somewhere else, storing it for private personal use. So all the rest of us get the leftover bad weather nonstop."

"Disgusting," said a woman who had come to Peshamba with her three daughters.

"Disgusting," echoed Daughters Number One and Two.

Number Three, the youngest, said flirtatiously to Argul, "Umm . . . would you pass the bread please?"

"Perhaps my wife can," said Argul graciously, "as she's nearer."

So I passed the youngest daughter the bread, which she accepted with quite a glare.

Despite everything, I was startled when Argul called me his *wife*. Although by then I was.

We'd gotten married that afternoon. Argul said afterward, when we came out of the wedding-building, "Did something *happen* in there?" Because the wedding had been—well, actually AWFUL. Which was another reason why, right then, I didn't write about it. But now that I'm writing in this book again, I might as well.

Argul had said that marriages took place at Peshamba under the CLOCK-which-is-a-god. But it turns out that's only for Peshambans, or people who have lived in the town at least a year. I suppose it's quite fair really. But very disappointing. What I'd remembered about Peshamba most, aside from its jewel-colors, was its generosity to outsiders.

The first time we'd tried to get married I had been kidnapped by the Wolf Tower and then re-kidnapped by Ironel's men, and the WT told Argul I'd left him to go off with that creep Nemian, which luckily Argul didn't believe. The *second* time we were supposed to get married was in the Raven Tower at Chylomba, where Twilight Star wanted to see us swiftly hitched and then bred like two pedigreed wolves. Yuk. We had escaped that one.

The third marriage should have been special, to make up for the mess before.

It wasn't special. It was mostly just *quick*.

First we were sent to a building with a red dome, where we had to sign a paper which said we wished to marry. There was no one in the room as we did this. Then a doll came in.

I'd gotten used to the life-sized moving dolls at the Rise, especially one doll, Jotto, who was remarkably unmechanical and *human*. Then there had been that other doll on the way to Chylomba—whose only virtue had been its total believable reality.

Ustareth and Twilight Star could/can make dolls of that type. Now Peshamba's dolls, which had seemed so astounding the first time I'd seen them, looked very stiff and machine-ish.

This one wore a long, tubular robe of metallic silk and had a silver mask-face, and a high, round hat like a sort of halo, made of some kind of black wood.

I often speak to dolls and machines as if they're people, but this one I didn't. I just stood there, and the doll in the black halo-hat glided up to us.

"Do you have witnesses or friends?" it asked.

Argul said we didn't.

"Follow me," said Halo-Hat.

We followed it into a little bare room with a narrow table. The doll stood on one side.

We stood on the other side.

"What are your names?" We said them. "Are you free to marry?" We said we were.

Being a machine, it could somehow probably tell if we spoke the truth (?) and weren't two entirely other people, already married, or wanted for murder, etc.

Then it said to repeat what it said. And what it said was basically this: I, Claidi/Argul, swear that, by the laws of Peshamba, and in the sight of all gods whether or not believed in, I, Claidi/Argul am, from this hour, the wife/husband of Argul/Claidi, and shall so remain until such ties shall be undone.

When we'd both said our version of this, Halo-Hat said, "Now Peshamba pronounces you wife and husband, husband and wife."

And that was it. Oh, apart from paying for the "wedding" in another room.

"Do you feel married?" Argul said, as we stood on the mosaic stairway outside, and the cold air tinkled down the street.

I thought, and answered truthfully, "I felt married to you since the first, really—I mean since the first time we were here."

"Yes," he said. "That's all right then." He kissed me. "That goes for me as well."

"Peshamba was so beautiful then. I wish this had been— *then*."

He said, "Like I say, you can't go back, Claidi-baa."

Then we walked along to the square with the CLOCK.

And as we stood looking up at it nostalgically, we saw that it had icicles like needles pointing all down the length of its high tower. The gold and silver of the CLOCK-frame was tarnished from cold, and the daylight figures—girl, young man, winged unicorn—seemed somehow spoiled.

There was some scaffolding up, too, and when Argul asked a passing man about it, we heard the frost had affected the mechanisms—the figures currently visible didn't move any more, and the night-time ones had been unseen for several nights.

It was enough to make anyone frown, particularly a Peshamban. Probably it explains, more than the weather, why no one much seems to be smiling.

We went and had some spicy mulled wine to cheer us up. How dreadful. The marriage ceremony had been such rubbish, we needed cheering up.

And there was no one with us, no Dagger, Teil, Blurn, to have a party with. And we weren't in the mood for a party really.

We—I—tried not to be surly, resentful, or angry.

We went back to the room-house, and behaved like two responsible adults to whom it didn't matter that one of the most important events of their lives had just been wrecked.

And like two responsible adults we'd gone down to dinner.

But then, when Argul said "*My wife*" showing the flirty youngest daughter that he was with me—*that* was when I felt a kind of glorious sunrise inside me.

Later, I thought, we have so much, it would be crazy to fuss about something so unimportant as that clockwork marriage.

✦ ✦ ✦

The thing is, though, now that I sit here in our rented room, writing in my book under the window, and outside the frosty day goes on (Number 39 Frosty Day, for now almost everyone here is keeping count)—the thing is, I've had this thought: What if the marriage *itself* has become clockwork.

What do I mean?

I mean, Argul and I—our relationship—is it just running along automatically, but the feeling has—changed—*frosted over* in some way? So it's working on the surface, but not as it *should*. This is awful. I'm being extra dumb. . . . We're *happy*. It's just that there's a shadow on us, of what was there before and has gone. What Argul gave up, what I know he misses, perhaps all the time, even when we're joking and laughing, even when I'm in his arms and he in mine. Even then?

And I can't be sure.

This small vast area of himself he keeps apart from me, shielding me, I think, from any depression he feels.

Does he feel depressed?

I know he does.

There was all the excitement and rush before—pursuit, escape—but now, everything's done.

I should have kept Yinyay. She's in his pocket. If she'd been in mine, I could have called her up to me-size, and talked to her. If I ask for her—he'll know I need someone else to confide in.

Am I being unreasonable?

I don't know enough.

After the wedding, I thought we'd take straight off again, traveling in Yinyay. But he said, "Why don't we stick around here until the weather improves?" As if *weather* could matter to us, with a flying Tower—but that's just it, it would matter, if we were living normal lives, Hulta lives.

I said, "Yes, let's wait."

So now nothing changes. Clockwork days, clockwork repeating frosts. Clockwork us, making clockwork jokes and clockworkily in love. *No!*

?

He kept a couple of books real-sized when Yin shrunk herself and everything. He sits, reads those. Or we go for lots of walks. Stare at things. Come back here. But today he said he wanted to go for a walk alone. He was smiling, almost playful as he said this, and I thought, *He wants to get away from me, by himself, to think.*

So I said, "Yes, that's a good idea, I'd like to buy some things here. I'll do that better on my own."

We have money, too, of course, from Yinyay. We have everything from Yinyay. And he knows I'm safe with the Power ring. And he wants not to be with me.

Our lazy life, and nothing to do at all. He's used to doing things, *being. Living*—

Is this my fault?

Oh hell, I don't know what to do.

When I go down, the fur coat girl is lurking by the front door.

"We," she says to me, accusing, "don't like this weather. It's not good for trade."

She thinks the *weather* is my fault?

I've gotten in such a state by then, I almost wonder if it is.

THE GROVE OF MASKS

All over Peshamba there are large public gardens—parks. Wandering around, I found a new one.

I'd bought some silk in a market, for a dress, and a smart bronze and iron cookpot—neither of which I/we need, since Yinyay supplies everything. (Yes, it *can* be frustrating, I ungratefully admit.)

The park was dim and cold.

The lawns had been burnt by the frost, which still iced the edges of every blade. All the trees were bare, even the palm trees (very odd *they* looked), except there were a lot of evergreens, the kind that grow even in winter temperatures, pines, cedars, holly, bay trees.

I ambled around a pond, which had been broken free of

ice in the middle for some fed-up-looking ducks. I didn't see many other birds, or anything much. Everything was in hiding.

Had the thing about the good weather being stolen been possible?

I thought about the country of Winter in the north. Was that endless snow climate natural? Twilight and the Raven Tower were pretty powerful, and their technology was awesome. But could they reach down here, so far into the south?

Venn's mother, Ustareth, is the only other one who could have done something like that, I bet. But I know Ustareth died nine years ago. She was Argul's mother, too, and he saw her buried when he was ten years old.

Which ought to be a relief, but somehow isn't, because she seems to have cast her shadow over us forever. Over everyone, with all those games and plots and tests she left for us all to struggle with and trip over.

I glanced around, and stopped.

I'd meandered away from the pond, and was now in a kind of little wood of firs and other trees with leaves.

Through the trees ahead, I glimpsed a formal-looking procession of people. They looked really peculiar, and in fact, they had stopped quite still, and—oh yes, they weren't people, but bizarre statues—!

I went between the trees, and out onto a small cropped lawn the evergreens surrounded.

Of course I'd seen statues in all sorts of areas, including Peshamba. But none like these.

There were several stone-robed figures, with masks. Some

had masks of black enamel and a couple had stone hoods. These reminded me of the priests of the Moon Temple in the marshes that lie between here and the City of the Towers. Next there was a tall, female-looking figure in a dark blue stone gown, with a face-mask of palest silver. Others had hats. They were all very tall—about eight feet—and narrow but for the carved flow of their stony clothes. The light caught on all the masks, of enamel, silver, or polished brass. None of the masks had proper features, just a suggestion of nose, mouth, eyes. (The eyes, because they were of the same stuff as the rest of the mask, looked closed.) The faces were beautiful but completely noncommunicative. There was nothing friendly about them. In fact, they seemed sinister.

Then I thought I saw someone coming and looked up, and across the lawn, standing among the jade green bay trees, were three more figures, one with a round black halo-hat, and one with a hat like a translucent green melon, and the third with a hat like an upside-down gold umbrella.

They hadn't, of course, moved. They'd been there all the time, but I hadn't seen them at first, until a little frozen wind stirred the branches.

What a weird place.

Then I saw a stone standing to one side and only being a stone. There were some words painted on it, and they were in Peshamban, but Argul had taught me a bit of that. The lettering read *Mask Grove*.

I walked all around all the statues. I found another pair in among the trees, with *copper* round halo-hats.

Masks are worn a lot in Peshamba. The grove was all right, I supposed. I just didn't like it.

If today had been sunny, and flowers out—it might have looked different, maybe.

I sat on the painted stone, to do my thinking, anyway.

One of the things I'd written in this book, before I picked it up again today, was how I wanted to go and try to get Daisy, Pattoo, and Dengwi—at least—out of the filthy House. D, P, and D had been my friends. I've often wondered what became of them after my Escape with Nemian into the Waste-which-wasn't.

And here was some action—something valuable to do. A Quest even. The Quest to Rescue D, P, and D.

The moment Argul got back to the room, I would put this to him. He wouldn't say No.

And the one great thing was that, with our Power jewelry and Yinyay the Tower, we should have absolutely nothing to worry about regarding the defenses or viciousness of the House. Even the House Guards wouldn't stand a *chance*. And if nothing else, seeing *that* would be fun.

I felt better. Carrying my parcels I got up, nodding to the statues, thinking I was glad they couldn't move.

The wind was getting rough as I marched up the lawns. It rushed harshly through the longer grass of the park, and scraped the bare branches overhead. Up in the blank sky some clouds had appeared, big and dark.

When I came out on the streets again and turned toward the room-house, I was glad Peshamba is so easy to find your way around. That's partly because all the streets have such memorably obvious names (for example, the street with the wedding-building is called Marriage Street).

There weren't many people out, and those that were were scurrying along like the winds, no doubt trying to get indoors before whatever unpleasant new weather was coming hit the town.

Very oddly though, the scurriers still spared some very wild glances for me. Some even halted a moment, gaping, and then usually they crossed the street. What on earth—?

It wasn't until I got to Loaf Street (where they make a lot of bread) that, squinting against the now-driving wind, I realized that the people I met weren't actually staring at *me*. No, they were staring behind me.

So then, I too hesitated, turned, and—
STARED.

They were all there. Even some I hadn't spotted before. The masked statues from the grove.

When I stopped and turned, they stopped, too, quite still.

I gave a wail. The wind carried it away.

I took one step, cautiously, backward, then another.

The statues all came rolling forward several inches.

They seemed to be moving on invisible wheels; certainly they didn't take actual steps. Their stone clothes stayed perfectly rigid. No expressions, or gestures.

But they had followed me from the park, and now they seemed all set to continue to follow me wherever I meant to go—

Of course, I panicked.

I flung around again. Staring hadn't answered any questions, and walking backward hadn't fooled them. I ran.

Short distances, I can run quite fast. So I bolted through the streets of Peshamba, with the freezing now-gale of a wind trying to push me either over on my face or flat on my back. And whenever I turned, they were still there.

All the time, even at that speed, my head was buzzing with *Why? Why??*

By the time I got to the CLOCK square, I'd had this unwelcome memory of various horror-stories I've read or been told, where some dupp insists on entering the forbidden mansion or temple, reads the dire warning DO NOT DISTURB, and gleefully disturbs *everything*. Then gets upset when the local vengeful ghoul or ghost hurtles in pursuit.

But all I'd done was look at the blasted statues. And . . . thought that I was glad they *couldn't* move. Had they read my mind and taken it as a challenge?

And then I thought of the diamond ring, which I'm still not used to, nor all the curious magics it can perform.

Blundering to a muddled stop in the middle of the square, me and my procession now extremely gawped at by shopkeepers busy shutting doors, and men scrambling on the CLOCK scaffolding, I spun around and confronted the statues.

I shook my hand at them—the hand with the ring.

The ring, whatever else, would protect me. If it had managed to keep me safe from Twilight's attempt to murder me, this was nothing.

"Stop and stay still," I ordered the statues. "No further."

Then I turned resolutely and strode off across the square. I was less confident than desperate.

However, sure enough, when I got to the square's other side and looked back again, *they* had stayed rooted to the paving. There were at least twelve of them.

People were coming out into the cloud-dark wind, swinging down off the scaffolding, hurrying over to the statues to look at them, then pointing after me, *really interested.*

Claidi strikes again.

Maybe it's my maid-slave years in the House that so often convince me evasion is the best policy. I took to my heels.

When I reached the room-house, thankfully alone, I dashed in and straight upstairs.

The moment I got through the door, the wind from outside, which had somehow also gotten in and was now warm, heavy and hairy, leaped hard against me and knocked me back against the wall.

"Yaah—!—a wolf!"

"Only half of him," said Argul, standing there, grinning.

"It's a dog!"

It was a dog.

The dog was very large, and obviously friendly, or the ring wouldn't have let him near me. He had liquid muscles rippling under a flapping coat of coarse white and grey fur. Two eyes rimmed in black fur beamed yellow-amber *down* into mine, as the dog stood there with his front paws placed squarely on my shoulders, before washing my face thoroughly with one pink swipe of his tongue.

"I think he wants to dance with you," observed Argul.

"Yes, he's not very good though, he's already stepped on both my feet."

"He must have broken several toes."

"At least. Yes," I added to the dog, as he laughingly snorted, "you're very handsome. But should we sit this one out? Whose is he?" I added.

"Ours."

"Oh—ours?"

"I've had him on order for days."

"Sorry?"

"And two horses," Argul said. "The elephant-seller. He sells other animals, too. But the weather here held everything up. This dog is a thoroughbred wolfhound cross. They can be the best. I had a dog like this one when I was a kid. The horses are good stock, too, northern bred. Wait till you see. I know I probably should have let you choose your own this time, but once I saw them, I really thought you'd like her. I chose Sirree for you, remember. She's a bit like Sirree. I wanted to surprise you. A wedding present."

The dog was still standing with his front paws on my shoulders. I thought, *We don't need horses, but we* need *them in another way.* This, too, was going to help make things better. So long as none of the animals minded being in Yinyay when they had to be.

Outside the wind hammered the roof; darkness was coming early. Unbothered, the dog touched my nose with his very *wet* nose.

"What's his name?"

"I haven't named him. What do you think?"

"Argul—*thank* you for doing this. He's lovely. It's all lovely." I threw my arms around the dog and buried my face in his fur, determined not to cry.

Argul said, "I'm sorry it was such a lousy wedding. But the wedding is only a formality. Like you said."

"*Yes*. It wasn't—that doesn't—I'm just—"

"Claidi," he said, when the three of us had sat down together on a rug, "I'm always going to remember and miss them, the Hulta. But it's you I want and have to be with, right?"

"Yes. Only you seemed—far off."

"It wasn't that so much. I was thinking of—" he paused, and said, "my mother. Zeera—Ustareth—whatever. I was thinking about when she died."

The dog and I both looked at him. Inevitably he would think of her after what we had come to know.

Argul said, "I was remembering how she went off one day by herself, and then she came back. That often happened, but this time—was different. She said she was ill, there was no known cure. She wouldn't have anyone near her. Not my father. Not me. None of the women even. And then she called us in, alone, one by one. Like dying royalty."

"She was," I said softly, "she *was* royal, Argul. She was from the Wolf Tower. So you are—like the wolf-dog—half."

"That's nothing," he said dismissively. His face was as bleak as the sky had been before the hectic eruption of the storm. "When I went in, she didn't say she was ill, just told me she had to go away. That was how she described it, death. Going away. She said she didn't want to go, but had no choice. I said—I said would she miss me? I was only ten. She said she would. Later on no one at all was allowed into her wagon. She told them to come back on the third morning. When they did, it was over. She knew all about herbs, medicines. She must have known what to do."

"Argul."

"She was brave," he said. "So brave no one knew what it really cost her. She was—*businesslike* about it. She didn't even cry. She left instructions for her burial, too. Everything was done how she wanted it. Goes without saying. She always got her way. Except over having to die."

Lightning splintered, and the dog turned and growled fiercely at the window. Hail slashed down the pane. Argul smoothed the dog's head. "He's brave, too, you see? He wants to fight the weather." I could see the hailstones; some were as big as chickens' eggs. Argul said, "Shall we call him Thu? It's the name of one of the thunder gods the Hulta have. We say the thunder happens when he stamps his feet because they get cold, and so you have to light your lamps and fires to warm him." He smiled, and the dog wagged his tail. The other conversation was over.

As we were lighting lamps and Thu was chomping on a bone Argul had brought for him, someone knocked on the door.

Argul said it might be the woman who rented out the rooms, come to make sure we had properly storm-proofed this one. Some people apparently throw open the windows, to "invite" a storm in. (?)

But when I opened the door, there stood one of the masked statues from the grove.

Perhaps not very rational now, I yelled at it, "How dare you come up here! Go back to the square at once!" Then, when it didn't obey me, really unnerved again, I gave it a shove.

The statue rocked on its runners.

"Do no harm in Peshamba, Peshamba does no harm to you," it moaned.

Argul was there, between me and it. (He forgets about the ring, too.)

"What do you want?"

The figure felt inside a flap of its robe. Which was of tubular metallic silk, not stone. The silver mask and round halo-hat had fooled me. It wasn't a statue, only a Peshamban doll, from Marriage Street.

"Here is your certificate of union," said the doll.

It held out to us a quite exquisite paper, hand-painted all over with colored flowers and birds, and even scented in some way, bearing a most wonderful almost-poem about how Argul and I were now legally joined in the sight of men, gods, and Peshamba.

"It has taken longer to prepare than usual," said the doll, "due to the frost's affecting the artist's paints. May you be always happy together."

Then turning itself round, it went rather bouncily off down the stair, while Argul, Thu, and I peered at it, astonished, over and through the bannister.

The next morning, the weather had changed again. It was still cold, but windless, and the sky was blue as those flowers the House called Forget-me-nots (and the Hulta called Remember-mes).

We were out early, and the elephant-seller took us on a tour of his animals, kept in the park by the Travelers' Rest. The elephants were gigantic—I'd only ever seen such creatures in the distance before, and then not believed what I was told about them. But they really do have sort of tail-noses. Also, they were now shedding off a kind of wool they'd put on in the frosts. The air was full of it, a soft fine snowfall after all.

Thu goggled, but didn't make a fuss. "His mother used to sit with the elephants sometimes. They're noble beasts," the seller told us.

Our horses were all ready, groomed and gleaming in the re-born sun. The horse Argul had picked out for himself was a tall, wide-chested animal, smooth dark tea-color, and maned in black silk—like Argul! So I said they matched. The horse he'd found for me was a black mare, truly like Sirree, but with white strands in her mane and tail, and one white front leg, that looked as if it had come through a hole in her otherwise black clothes. I loved her at once, and she has a beautiful nature. When we took them out, oh, that was—We mounted up and galloped for miles over the meadows around Peshamba, and birds, who had been there all the time, were flying up like golden bullets from the grass, singing, into the air.

"Look, Argul, there are flowers coming back!"

It was a fact. By afternoon, when we rode into the town again, I saw buds on most of the trees, like little sticky hard jewels of swarthy green and red.

So it was all going to be all right.

If it had been witchcraft, or someone stealing the weather (!?), it's stopped.

The figures on the CLOCK are also all right again. We saw them move tonight.

Tonight, too, Argul and I went for a baked marrow supper on Marrow Lane (where they bake marrows). And they told us this was free, the whole meal. Apparently the first one you order after you marry is on the town. This was nice, as the painted certificate had been.

So the wedding wasn't as cramped and mean as we'd thought. In fact, it was rather public—since they somehow tell the eating-places.

Tomorrow, we'll be leaving. We'll use Yinyay again, once we're clear of Peshamba. The going is too slow and treacherous for horses between here and the House, as I have cause to remember. A large part is desert.

Argul has agreed that we should try to rescue Daisy and Pattoo and Dengwi.

Thu barked when we called Yinyay up to doll-snake size this evening, in our room. But when Yinyay produced a dog biscuit with a chocolate covering, Thu decided Yinyay was actually the best thing to happen since dogs were invented.

How the horses take to the Yinyay Tower will be another matter.

It's late now.

"Come to bed, Claidi-baabaa," says Argul. Thu jumps on the bed at once and wrestles with Argul.

Everything, after all, seems—great.

I just looked out of the window before blowing out the

last lamp. May as well note that half the trees in the garden over the wall are blossoming, white in the light of a pale-moony street-lamp. At the wall's corner, a shadow flickered. It was very tall, with a halo-shaped hat above a glimmer of metal face— Then it was gone. Oh come on, Claidi. An official Peshamban doll, that's all. The statues from the Mask Grove have all been taken back there by now, must have been, since they weren't in the square when we were tonight.

The ring stopped them. But . . . did the ring somehow start them, too???

I don't want to think of the ring now, or Ustareth, who made it. Brave, clever, bossy, frightening, tragic Ustareth, who "had to go away."

Perhaps all the blossoms will be out in the morning, in time for us to see before we leave.

AT HOME

Yinyay, of course, could easily locate the House, and most (all?) places. And she had fashioned overnight a stable for the horses, a really smart affair, with straw and hay and the right kind of food. (Somehow she herself seems to manufacture all this—I don't understand how, or from what, and ages ago, when I asked her, she said something about *atoms* and *molecules*, as with her growing and shrinking—and lost me.) Perhaps not surprisingly, both horses took to their Tower stable at once.

I did wonder, when Yinyay went soaring up in the air, how they'd feel about that. We stayed with them, in case. But—they took no notice. Really there's hardly any sensation of flight or movement, and not much of going up and down. You'd only know that something was happening from looking out of the windows, and the stable doesn't have those.

Yinyay assured us that she would watch over the horses at all times. Like a wise nurse with two nervous moms, she added to Argul and me that if the horses seemed troubled, she'd let us know immediately.

Thu meanwhile had watched Yinyay get big with adoring admiration and tail-wagging. (She gave him another biscuit just before she did it. Perhaps he hoped, now she was huge, she'd give him a bigger biscuit.)

When we went inside, though, Thu forgot everything, even us, in his mad excitement to see and find everything. He galloped up and down the stairs, got into the lifts (yes, Yinyay has lifts) which obligingly opened for him as for us, tore around the living rooms, bedroom, and library, barking and snorting. He ended up in the plant-room, which is like an indoor garden, fully stretched on a lawn Yinyay has made, and which she assured us (him?) is fine for burying bones. She's even arranged a type of bathroom for him. He can even have a bath, if he wants one!

It seems odd to be traveling back across those landscapes I went through before, on the ground, first with Nemian, then with the Hulta.

From the upper air, everything is changed, unrecognizable.

Also, sometimes Yin probably takes a slightly different route.

Nem and I got lost, and the Hulta always wander. It was when they wandered to Peshamba that Nemian got his bearings, unfortunately, and dragged me off through the marshes to his City.

But I don't regret that, not now. If I ended the evil rule of the Wolf Tower Law, then it was worth it. Though I still don't entirely know, from what I've heard since, if I did.

I thought, I know those hills.

They look parched white from the air, desolate, rather like a model of hills made by someone not very inspired.

Engrossed, I stared down from the library window, remembering how the Sheepers had bartered me to the Feather Tribe hereabouts, who would have thrown me off a cliff as a Lucky Sacrifice, if Argul and Blurn hadn't rescued me. (Nemian had been useless, naturally.)

So did I feel strange? Oh, yes.

Then I saw that desert, which really is a Waste. It opened out on every side to the horizon's edge. Like a tray of some yellow-brown spice no one ever buys because no one likes it.

Now I was seeing the landscape I'd crossed the very first of all—*before I met Argul*. Now I was truly dropping backward into my past. My horrible, hopeless past, at the House.

I felt a wave of—almost fear. That startled me. I had *nothing* to fear now. Well, nothing physical. They couldn't hurt me now.

Only . . . will they remember me? I don't mean the princes and princesses and ladies and gentlemen—I doubt if *they* will, having never really seen me in the first place, all those sixteen years I was there. I mean my friends. That I had deserted. Forgotten. No, not exactly, but—

More than a year has passed since I left. Not so very long?

Will they in fact *remember* me, but not *want* to remember me?

Claidi, who ran away to freedom and happiness, and didn't look back.

This afternoon we landed briefly. We'd been flying quite slowly, and lowish, looking out. So when we saw this strange thing below in the desert waste, we just leisurely circled it and then went down to take a proper look.

When I was in this same desert before, there was a sandstorm (a total nightmare) which uncovered part of a sunken city. Presumably some other sandstorm had uncovered the gate.

That's what it was, you see. A gate. Or it might have been a doorway. Nothing else remained but a few shards of broken wall on either side of it and some litter on the dust-powdery ground.

It was very still there. Not a trace of wind, or even air. The sky darkest blue.

The gate towered up about thirty feet, five man-heights tall. It was made of a sort of brown stone, and the high-up entrance was arched. But on top of that was a shape like a quarter moon on its back, with—

"What a scary thing."

"Meant to be," Argul commented.

"Have you ever seen anything like it?" I asked. The Hulta of course are always widely traveled.

But "No," he said.

What was on top of the gate was an eye. No, an *Eye*.

It seemed to be made of polished pale marble, and maybe glass, unless they (whoever *they* were) had somehow found a green-blue jewel of that size, because the colored part of the Eye seemed at least as big as a cartwheel. It had a burnished black pupil, too. And all of it was clasped in two brown stone lids, upper and lower.

The Eye shone dully, fixedly staring away and away.

I said, "Perhaps it's another sort of watcher. Like at Peshamba and the other big towns. Like the City, and Chylomba—"

We stood, staring up at it, even Thu, who had come with us, as *it* stared off into the distance, and then—

Then the two lids slowly blinked, and the whole Eye moved—and was looking down, right at us.

I heard Argul curse.

My hair stood on end, and so did Thu's. He was growling.

But from the ring, nothing. No defensive flash. And nothing from Yinyay nearby.

So this wasn't an attack. It must only be what I'd said. The Eye in the high gate was a watcher, and it was *watching*.

Nevertheless, we did walk off slowly and kind of sideways. We kept our eyes on the Eye until we got back to Yinyay.

I called up to her then, "What is it? Is it trouble?"

Yinyay only then looked over, herself, from all her stories up, higher certainly than the gate.

She said, "I do not think it causes trouble. I do not know what it is."

I thought Yinyay knew *everything*.

Anyway, we got back inside and her doors shut, and Thu bounded upstairs as if demons were after him.

As we rose again into the air, we saw the Eye was now watching our ascent. When we sailed right over, it revolved completely upward, in a rather repulsive way, to see where we were going.

Neither Argul nor I was quite comfortable until it vanished over the horizon. Thu didn't appear until dinnertime.

We have reached the House.

It's there, standing in its miles of high-walled Garden, just as I recall.

This is how Nemian must have seen it first, drifting here in the balloon, before he got too near and the House Guards unpacked the cannon and blasted him out of the sky.

We *haven't* gone that near. We parked out on a rocky area about half a mile away.

No one seemed to notice our arrival.

The House never had watchers. And let's face it, the Guards were all star twonks.

Really, there are no signs of anything going on there at all, just a sunset blooming over behind the fortressed walls, rose-hip red.

I saw them last at dawn, with sunrise on them from the other direction.

Some birds just circled up, and settled down again, inside.

Yinyay says the river, which goes through the Garden, runs

under these rocks. She says, although it looks as if no one is at home, the House is packed with people.

We sat at a table, Argul and I.

"How do you want to handle this?" he asked me.

"Oh, I'll—well, the way I said."

"Right."

But I'm not sure now. I'd had it planned. Even asked Yin to make me a showoff dress. And now that seems ridiculous.

"I think we should wait until morning," Argul said. "Visitors at night may cause an overreaction."

"Yes, that's probably best."

In the morning I decided to put on the dress after all. It was made of the Peshamban silk I'd bought, light crimson and embroidered with peach-colored flowers and silver beads. It was *not* the garment of a maid-slave of the House, nor like any of the stupid House fashions.

Really, though I refused to admit it, I'd known I would feel like this, coming back here. I felt like a servant without rights, again. I felt like the child who'd been pushed for punishment into the Black Marble Corridor, where eerie winds whined through "cleverly" positioned holes, and there were pictures in oils of weeping exiles cast from the House into "Hell" outside. I now knew that everything they said about Hell was lies. I knew so much more than I ever had. And I was with Argul. And I had Yinyay and the ring and—well. I was still afraid I was going to feel one foot tall and seven years old, the moment we got inside the Garden walls.

We'd agreed not to take Thu. My ring would protect me, and though Argul's sapphire didn't defend him the same way, it still gave him flight, could open doors, windows, and so on.

Though alert for any violence, he seemed to have no insecurity. Why should he? He was born free and grew up a king and a warrior. He is, though he always dismisses it, a prince of the Towers.

Part of my Plan had been not to attempt any Invasion Tactics (part of why Yinyay was parked some way off). I felt we couldn't dive in and try to snatch Daisy and the others. There were a lot of people here, and there might be undeserving casualties.

We walked to the Front Door.

Oh yes, the House has one. I'd never known, when I lived there. Yinyay had told me that morning.

Did they ever *use* the Front Door? Maybe not, since for decades no one went outside—except when exiled. Then, I suppose.

Nemian and I got out through the tunnels under the Garden, with the help of all the keys the Old Lady Jizania gave me.

Now the Front Door would almost certainly open, not from a key, but from our scientific jewelry.

The sun lit the stonework. I could smell trees, flowers, from inside. And then a whiff of hippo from the river.

The Door was a big oblong, set between pillars, lofty enough so that you could walk through it even if you were nine feet tall.

It was shut, obviously.

We stood and waited.

After a moment, I thought, *It isn't going to open.*

Then I heard the locks grating, unused for years, cranky, which is why they took so long to respond.

Grumbling, grinding, the Front Door of the House yawned slowly wide.

And there before us lay the lush lawns of the Garden, and the river sparkling in the sun between the blades of reeds and purple irises.

It was lovely, just the way I'd suddenly realized it was, that time before I left.

Argul stepped through first, making sure. But there was nothing to fear in such a heavenly place. Unless you were a servant or a slave.

Going along those dainty paths, through those little woods, by those grottoes of carefully arranged, picturesque fake ruins was one of the weirdest things I've ever done.

Neither Argul nor I spoke. Though sometimes we turned to look—at that rosy bird fluttering into a tree, and that hare leaping away into a clovery orchard of ripening cherry trees. He didn't offend me by saying, *It's quite nice, isn't it, here.* But *I* offended me by thinking it.

Well. It is.

It's beautiful. Always was. If you were allowed to enjoy it.

We'd been striding along for about three-quarters of an hour, when we heard voices, and I thought, *Ah, some delightful icky lords and ladies,* from the jolly sounds.

We were on a path with huge tall yew hedges on either

side, cut in shapes like stars and birds and things, and to my extra surprise, I couldn't quite remember where this path led. Probably hadn't been so far out in the Garden that often—most of my tasks, and the rituals, had involved places nearer the House.

I paused. No, let's be honest, I froze.

Now I thought any sort of Plan would be better than the one I'd devised. I mean, we could have gone over the Garden at night, unseen. Positioned ourselves where we could see the House, looked out for Pattoo and the others the next day—then cunningly approached them, persuaded them, carried them off through the sky if necessary . . . provided the Power jewels could cope with their extra weight.

Only all that could have taken ages. And I wasn't sure about the weight thing. I'd tried flying with some heavy books and couldn't get very high up. And Daisy was quite light, while Pattoo and Dengwi were both bigger, although in different ways. Dengwi was my height and slim, and Pattoo shorter but heavier. Argul could manage, but could I? The *books* had made my arms ache. And then we'd probably have to leave at least one person behind and go back for them, and might get seen, or *they* might get stopped—

You can see.

My final Plan, however, was insane.

I simply meant to march in and ask—tell them—what I wanted. Use my Authority, as ghastly Lady Twilight would no doubt have said. *She'd* have thought I could do it, for sure. And I was relying, too, on the fact that Jizania Tiger would know who I was, what I'd done, and that I might be *very* dangerous.

Which had seemed all right until now.

I glanced at Argul. He hadn't put on particularly showy clothes. He doesn't even dress Hulta much anymore, not since we were in the north. He was peering through a gap in the hedge some way above my head.

"What can you see?" I hissed.

A gust of eversomerry mirth pranced up from beyond the walk.

"Several men and women playing a game with sticks, some little colored balls, and small arches stuck in the ground."

"Oh, that's Mallet," I said. I pulled a face. Lords and ladies definitely. "They're royal."

"They look it. Royal and rich."

"Are you ready?" I asked him.

He met my gaze. "Are *you?*"

"I'm—trying to be. But I think it'll take longer than we've got."

"They'll just run in terror," he said, "when they get blinded by that dress of yours."

This, from a Hulta—who feel naked without fringes, tassels, horsebells, coins. Then he laughed. Out loud. An easy, musical *Argul* laugh. (Curious, his voice *is* musical, though *not* when he sings.)

But I realized he'd stopped my panic. Also that, deliberately, he'd let the tronkers around the hedge know that someone else was here.

Sure enough, Argul said, "They're all looking this way now. They don't seem nervous yet, but then they don't know it's you, Claidi-baari."

"Forward march, then."

And so we stalked out onto the lawn, I with my head held high and my eyes kept straight and ready as two arrows.

And the first person my arrow-eyes saw was Pattoo, in a bright, flowery *gold-trimmed* gown, standing there with her mallet-stick, interrupted in midsmile.

LION NIGHT

attooo?"

"Claiiidi?"

We teeter there, both of our mouths open in amazement.

Pattoo, dear, careful, overconcerned Pattoo, who tried never to get anything wrong—less from fear of our disgusting, easily offended mistress, Lady Jade Leaf, than from a basic Pattooishness—a *need* to do things correctly.

She looked great in her flowery dress. She had a gold butterfly pinned in her hair, too. I mean—it was *gold*.

"Pattoo—" (again).

"Claidi—" (again).

Someone giggled.

I pulled my eyes away and saw Flamingo, another maid

(though she hadn't belonged to Lady J), all done up in flamingo-pink, *hiccuping* with amusement.

Pattoo said, more calmly:

"How are you, Claidi? You do look well."

"*Well?* I'm *speechless!*" I shrieked. I then stared all around and took in the fine royal ladies and gents in their gorgeous clothes and ornaments. And they were all—all—ALL—servants.

And that woman, there, she was a *slave*, and that old man—who is now a distinguished, princely Old Man—used to be a slave, too.

I know he was. I recall once, when I was only a kid, I saw him beaten because he couldn't pull Prince Shawb's rotten chariot fast enough.

And now—he's in brocade, and he's sipping something from a silver hip-flask. Only when he grins, I see the gap of the tooth Shawb also personally knocked out.

Rather than running right at Pattoo and shaking her, to make sure she, and all of them, aren't a dream, I say firmly, "Pattoo, whatever has happened?"

"Oh, a lot," says Pattoo, flitting her big dark eyes up, down, at Argul. "To you, too, I think. Hmm."

They told me then. We sat down on the Mallet Lawn, and someone produced a basket with fresh fruit and yellow wine, and over this they explained.

I could *not* take it all in.

"But you say it was because of what I did?"

"Yes, Claidi. You and the Old Lady."

After a while, we'd eaten all the fruit and drunk all the

wine. Then they carefully put away the Mallet things in a small shed (their property now, so they look after it as well as they always did) and we walked up through the rest of the Garden toward the House.

Nearer, among the glasshouses and coldframes and grape arbors, lots of people were working, and when they looked up were told, "*Claidi's* come to visit."

It was a big house, the House. There were hundreds of us. We didn't all know each other, then, how could we have? It was the royal people we knew, we *had* to. And now I looked into faces I didn't recall, people I'd never met, or had only met as we were rushing to obey our owners, or crawling about scrubbing floors or something. And these unmet people, who had been servants and maids when I had been a maid, and who had been slaves, now left what they were doing and crowded around, as no servant or slave was ever at liberty to do.

"Is *this* Claidi?" "Yes, I *remember* Claidi." "Wow, this is CLAIDI!"

"Fame at last," said Argul.

He seemed at ease, but I knew he was keeping part of himself cool, silent, and on guard.

This was to have been another House of Enemies, where we must bluff and threaten our way, as we have so often before.

Had everything really changed here so much?

It seemed that it had.

They were still explaining. I was getting the hang of it at last.

By the time I suddenly saw, through a drift of daffodil

trees, the hated salmon and green structure of the House, I'd more or less come to believe what had happened here.

The Revolution.

They call that night Lion Night now. It's become a festival, which they celebrate at irregular intervals, really just when they feel like it. (Already they were saying it must be celebrated again tonight, in my honor.)

When I'd escaped with Nemian, who had been the House prisoner, it was late—after midnight?—I can't be sure, now. But no one was about, except the odd lion, because someone had also opened the lion house and let them out.

Anyway, Nemian and I went along the tunnels, got outside by breaking open the last door, and were in the desert.

Meanwhile, some other things took place.

Pattoo told me. Jizania had provided drugged wine, not only for the House Guards house-guarding Nem, but for *all* the House Guards. Various maids took it to the guard tower, and anywhere else they happened to be. Jizania sent a message that she wanted to reward the Guards for valiantly shooting down Nemian's balloon. Of course the twonksome guards always thought they were sensationally deserving, so they slurped the wine, and within ten minutes were out cold.

The first thing anyone knew about this was when some people ran into the Maids' Hall in the darkness, yelling and waking everyone up. These people were Jizania's servants, but at the time no one quite knew *who* they were.

Here is the story they told: Claidi had risked her life to rescue the captured Nemian, and had taken him to safety outside the walls. The House Guards were drugged, by Claidi and by others.

Then Jizania walked into the hall, without escort, and looking magnificent as always in her bald ancient beauty.

"Listen to me," said Jizania to the startled servants, and they listened. "Are you ready to be as brave as Claidi? If not," she added, "think how you will all be punished by your cruel and unjust masters. Do you think they'll stand for this, to be cheated of their prisoner by one of *you?*" And then Jizania had pointed all across the jostling, scared crowd. She'd pointed at Dengwi. "You," said Jizania harshly. "What will *you* do?"

"Dengwi just—she just leapt into action!" said Pattoo proudly. "She looked splendid, her hair flying and her eyes flashing in the unsteady lamplight—" (you can tell, like me, Pattoo had always been one to read stolen novels).

Still, Dengwi jumped up on a table and she yelled at every-one that the lords and ladies would probably now kill their ser-vants, and then they'd go after Claidi and kill her and the "innocent" Nemian. (Innocent—hah!) " 'Claidi is a heroine,' cried Dengwi," said Pattoo. " 'She was all alone. But think—to-gether with the slaves, we outnumber the royalty in the House by at least five to one.' "

At these explosive words, there was uproar.

"It was—fantastic!" reminisced Pattoo. She lowered her eyes. "But frightening."

Everyone had immediately run to the slave quarters. No one tried to stay quiet now; they were roaring and screaming, and they'd lit torches (like in the *best* over-the-top adventure novel) but mostly to see their way in the dark Garden now that the moon was down. The torches came in handy also when they met the lions roaming about, although they were fairly tame, for lions. But anyway Dengwi, now at the front of the Horde, shouted "These lions are the *sign*. We, too—are escaped lions!" Very rousing, naturally.

Then they marched on the House. (Honestly, there were hundreds of them—us—why had we never thought of this before?)

When Pattoo and the others told me all this, I wondered if what I heard next would be about a bloodbath.

We had hated our masters. We'd had every reason. Most were unkind, demanding, and uncaring. Many were monsters.

It was Flamingo who said to me, "We didn't kill anyone, Claidi. I mean, that's what *they* would have done to us. So we just *wouldn't*."

"What *did* you do?" I must have asked this several times. Or they told me several times.

Of course, what they did was Exile the lords and ladies, the princes and princesses.

Dengwi said to them, "The House is ours now. We know how it works and how to look after ourselves. We've been the ones who always kept everything running. It's you royalty who don't know how to survive. We've had to do it all for you."

She told them to get out. Oh yes, I can see her, splendid. All her blackness burning under the torches, and the fire in her eyes. Like a lion, yes.

The only thing is, I don't remember her like that. She was always rather quiet and, well, reserved. I suppose it was just the time making her do it, the situation. Strange, though, Jizania fixing on her like that. *You—what will YOU do—*

Even then, with the birds singing, and everyone so proud, I was thinking, there is more to this. . . .

However. Only the royals who simply begged to remain were allowed to stay. And then they mostly (there were only seventeen) lived like everyone else. They are allowed to have comfortable rooms, and they can have days off, but that's like everyone else now, and like everyone else, they too work.

"Lady Iris is a brilliant cook!" enthused Groother, who was one of the male slaves I'd known to talk to.

"Lady Iris was always all right," I agreed.

Someone said sternly we were both wrong; no one was called lord or lady any more.

Groother and I both apologized.

I thought then, and later—constantly—but why aren't they angry with me? I could have got them all hanged by what I'd (selfishly? Stupidly—unthinkingly) done. But they weren't angry. They liked me—for *making* them rebel. I was a symbol, like the lions.

But Jizania . . . She'd said to me, back then, over and over, how she was so old and bored, too tired to do very much. And yet she'd been as much the spark to touch off the powder keg as anyone. Of course, the royalty of the House had been the ones to kick Twilight, Jizania's daughter, out, with her beloved Fengrey, because they'd broken the House rules. So maybe Jizania had all that time been nursing this grudge, and then took the opportunity to pay them all back? Then there's Dengwi. Why had she been so *ready* to react?

I'd fallen for Jizania's act, fallen for a whole lot. Now I just suspected plots behind plots. My experience of the Wolf Tower has taught me to think like this. Perhaps I'm wrong. And perhaps I'm not.

I wanted to talk to Dengwi.

"And Jizania?" It was Argul who asked this lightly. "Did she stay on?"

"Oh, she stayed, of course. She'd helped us."

"All three Old Ladies stayed," said Groother. "The other two, Corris and Armingat, are useless, but they don't do any harm. We don't expect them to work at their age."

"We all take our turn with the work," said Flamingo virtuously.

"Even the nasty jobs are fine, now that we've got it all organized."

"And now no one stands over us with a whip."

I keep thinking, too, of how Nemian and I were still only just outside the walls all that night, because he was too lazy or princelike to want to move until sunrise. And *all that* was going on, only a few miles from us. Why hadn't we heard it? Surely the noise of the shouting, at least some of it, would have carried through that still night—some of the *electricity*—

No, we were both too wrapped up in ourselves to hear or sense it. And also I'd been wrapped up in the fact of Nemian, I regret to say, starry-eyed and a fool.

I could have gone back. That's the strangest thought. I mean, I could have just gone back to the House and been safe, and had a new life there, free and happy, with everyone and everything I knew around me. What would have happened if

I'd heard those shouts, seen the lights, been courageous enough to go to see? I would never have met Argul. Nothing would be as it is. Life is—mysterious.

"This is Dengwi's room."

It was impressive. It must have belonged to a prince or princess. More than one room, in fact. All vanilla pillars. There was an "antechamber" with paintings and drapes, and then a satin sitting room, with great big windows, and then a short corridor to the door of Dengwi's *private* room.

Pattoo, who'd brought us, left us in the sitting room, and went and knocked on the door up the corridor.

"Dengwi, are you there?" we heard her meekly call.

I've said, Dengwi was my friend. I'd thought of her like that. But I didn't really know her that well. Daisy, Pattoo, and I had shared a gossipy little cubbyhole at the Maids' Hall. Dengwi was in another room, with two other girls. What we had in common was we all served Lady Jade Leaf.

My last memory of Dengwi was when darling LJL promised to have me whipped professionally—instead of constantly hitting me with her cane that stung and drew blood. *"You mustn't be whipped,"* Dengwi had insisted to me. "My sister was, and—she nearly died." I hadn't known what to say (I'd been paralyzed with terror). Hadn't even known Dengwi had a sister.

I suppose Dengwi was always a little, well, not standoffish, more aloof. She was very poised, together. When Jade Leaf hit her, as Jade Leaf was always hitting and pinching and kicking all her servants, Dengwi might have been made of steel.

Now she walked out of her inner room and into this one, and I goggled.

Then I glanced at Argul. And I saw he was studying Dengwi in quite a new way. He'd been flirty and nice with the other girls, but now his manner altered. He seemed—even more alert.

She wore a plain white dress. But around her neck was a snake of sculpted gold. She had put back her hair in a gold net. She looked . . . powerful. And adult. That, I'd say, was always her quality anyway.

After what had happened, maybe the powerfulness wasn't surprising either. She'd led a revolution.

"Dengwi," said Pattoo, "it's Claidi."

Dengwi stood looking long at me. Fine. Was she going to say haughtily, "Who is Claidi?"

"And Argul," Pattoo explained, "Claidi's husband."

"Shouldn't that," said Dengwi quite softly, "be Nemian?"

All I thought of to do was shake my head.

How much did people here now know about the Wolf Tower? Perhaps nothing. But Jizania certainly knew things about the Wolf Tower, and there was something between Dengwi and Jizania. Oh yes.

"It's a long story," I added.

She didn't seem, as everyone else had, madly pleased to see me. Actually she looked, I thought with sudden dismay, *royal*.

Pattoo, the Faultless Hostess, murmured, "Claidi has come from Peshamba, a town to the south. It's very good to see her."

"Yes, indeed," said Dengwi.

(They didn't seem, no one had, dumbstruck at the idea

that there were towns and other areas of habitation out in the Waste. So decidedly that had changed, too.)

"Pattoo's told us," Argul said, conversational, "about the revolt here. Congratulations on your success."

Dengwi nodded. "We were lucky. And Jizania helped us."

I said, "And was it you who let the lions out?"

Dengwi's face relaxed. "Yes. I did that while Daisy and Pattoo and the others took the wine to the Guards."

"So everyone was in on it," I said, "but for me."

"Hardly everyone. Jade Leaf's maids, that's all. Jizania recruited us, you might say. She thought we were a good bet, since Jade Leaf was both vicious and stupid. It was arranged with us and her that evening, after she made plans with you."

"I didn't know." I stated the obvious.

Dengwi said, "She didn't mean you to. She wanted you to concentrate on getting Nemian away, and then both of you reaching his city."

So she does know about the Wolf Tower?

I felt it was wiser if I didn't bad-mouth Nemian to Dengwi, in case. Just as I hadn't Jizania, who'd sent me off to a new and much worse slavery under the Wolf Tower Law.

I was bewildered, though, almost insulted.

All that skulking around that night, and feeling so guilty about not telling Pattoo and the others. And—they were *ahead* of me, and not telling *me*.

I imagined Dengwi slinking through the shadows, fearlessly opening the lions' cage with another of Jizania's keys.

And Daisy and the rest, making eyes at the Guards as I'd had to, encouraging them to drink the wine.

"Let's sit down," said Dengwi, like a queen.

We sat.

Pattoo said, "They want to hold Lion Night tonight, in Claidi's honor. She's never been here before to enjoy it with us."

I beamed.

Argul beamed.

Wolf Tower plots were still possible. Had it not been the best idea after all to come here? Was this still a House of Enemies?

We weren't left alone all that day. Everyone kept coming to see us, as if we were an exhibit. Claidi and Argul Her Husband, from Peshamba. (We hadn't said from where else.)

They gave us guided tours of the House, showing us fancy apartments now turned into sewing-rooms and nurseries. (The Debating Hall had had its seats ripped out and had become a real exhibition, of devastating dullness—full of instruments of Servant Toil, such as brooms, hoes, clothes-brushes, etc. All carefully labeled so no one forgot what they were.)

People gushed up to us. Heroine and Hero. Perhaps they were just curious, or friendly, fellow-workers set free.

It all made me uncomfortable. I didn't think I deserved *praise* of all things for running off. And I kept wondering about plots. Jizania is Twilight's mother. That says everything.

I tried to see what Argul thought. Difficult. Between waves of people we had three-second dialogues. Like, Me: "Should we get out of here?" He: "We always can if we have to. There aren't any Guards now, are there? They were all kicked out." Me: "Yes, but something's going on—" Someone Else, abruptly arriving: "Oh, do come and see the roof pool. It used to be Kerp's roof garden, till we flooded it accidentally."

And later, while we were admiring the dismal stuff in the Debating Hall, I said, "No one needs rescuing here. We could just slip away." But Argul said, "There's still Jizania. Don't you want to meet her at this Dinner tonight?" "*Me?* Do *you* want to?" "I'm fascinated," he said.

And then we were swept off to watch a display of rug-cleaning by three former lords and a lady, who worrisomely, seemed genuinely thrilled at their deadly job.

Outside again, we came across the once-Lord Flindel, chopping wood for the Garden furnaces.

I recalled Lord Flindel. He had once tried to push me in the hippo river when he caught me stealing a flower. Now he greeted me cheerfully. Apparently he and I were old friends, too.

The Lion Night Dinner is always held on the lawns.

Everyone that can prepares it, arranges the tables, and so on.

The sun set ruby-red into the invisible desert. Ruby-red birds flew up like fireworks bursting from the trees, and wheeled around. They were once kept in the Aviary. But the freed slaves freed the birds. None of them fly away; they like it here.

Lady Iris, who was now just Iris, came sailing over the terraces to supervise all the dishes she'd made. She used to be quite large, but oddly, now that she cooks all the time, she's become quite slim.

Daisy was helping her at first.

I hadn't seen Daisy until then. Soon she rustled up in a tight-skirted dress patterned with daisies, and carrying a mustard pot. She was followed by a hulking male companion.

"Oh Claidi! I couldn't get away before." She hugged me to the mustard pot. The only one to dare—or want—to hug me. Then she ruined it. She said, "This is my boyfriend, Jovis."

It took me a minute to place him. Out of his Guard uniform he looked less important but also (impossibly?) less appetizing. He'd been one of the ones I'd drugged with the wine. Though he *had* hated Nemian, and wanted to behead him. Perhaps I could get to like Jovis—

Not appearing to bear a grudge about the drugging, he leered, then punched Argul heartily in the chest, and seemed disappointed when Argul didn't even sway.

"This your hubby? These women," confided Jovis loudly to Argul, "they keep on till they trap us, don't they? I expect *she'll*"—waving at Daisy—"want marrying soon."

"I had to work very hard to get Claidi to marry me," said Argul.

"Ah, yes, that's how they *manage* it. They make you think it's *you* doing the chasing."

"Really?" Argul was polite, interested to be educated. "I *see*."
Daisy frowned.

"Jovis," she snapped, "Iris says we have to hurry back and help with the centerpieces."

"There, you see," said Jovis, satisfied. "Nag, nag."

Off they went.

I wanted to spit.

Had Daisy no taste in men at all?

Then the moon rose.

It was three-quarters full and china white, and suddenly all the glamor of the Garden returned for me.

The tables were laid out along this one big area, the paved terrace below Hyacinth Lawn, where the great two-story-high waterfall plashes down and down.

Crystal glasses and cutlery glittered in the light of tall tangerine candles.

It reminded me of the Rise, even the sound of the waterfall, that evening we ate in the gardens there. Me and Treacle, that girl who could "cry" at will—enough to water the potted plants—and turned cartwheels to make us laugh, and splendid Grem, and kind mechanical Jotto—and . . . can you tell I've been putting off writing the last name?—and Venn.

Argul and I were actually alone for a moment. We watched the birds resettling in the trees.

"What is it?" he asked. "If you truly want to get out of here, let's just beat it."

"No, I think I do need to stay. I do need—to see Jizania again. And Dengwi. I need to sort this out if I can. Dengwi isn't my *enemy*, is she?"

"I think, from how she looked, she just got a shock when you turned up. And she's learned to hide things like that. It's like the way—" he hesitated.

"Like what?"

"Tell you later. Here comes Herself."

I looked where he was. "Jizania," I said. For here Herself was coming, and no mistake.

SPILLING THE BEANS

Before, she was supposed to be one hundred and thirty years old. So she must be going on a hundred and thirty-two by now. She looks so old, it isn't like Old any more. It's almost like a new kind of Young. She's probably the most beautiful woman I've ever seen. Even more beautiful than Winter Raven, who was disgustingly perfect.

Jizania Tiger wore an olive-green robe. Her hairless head was painted in complex spirals of gold and silver, with little gems pasted on. On her slender crooked wrist she carried her indigo bird. The big topaz ring dazzled on that hand, too. I'd forgotten about the topaz ring.

Of course, I thought instantly of the topaz Power ring at the Rise, which Ustareth had left there.

Was this one also Power jewelry?

I'd never seen or heard of her displaying supernatural abilities. But then Ustareth had hidden her own entirely successfully from the Hulta.

Then I got distracted.

At Jizania's side walked Dengwi. It was quite obvious they were companions. No Great-Lady-being-Patronizing-to-crawly-servant kind of thing.

And around them both, in a herd, padded about twenty lions.

Seems they're always let out on Lion Nights, in recognition of when they were let out before. They weren't on leads either.

I'd thought them tame, the lions, laid back and spoiled. But now, palely luminous in the moon and candlelight, black-maned, flame-eyed, they looked frankly fairly dodgy.

I had the feeling, though, even if they started leaping for everyone's throats, Jizania and Dengwi would be the last two people the lions would ever attack.

"Interesting," said Argul.

J, D, and lions were all moving straight toward us.

And now they were here.

Ignoring the big male lion that had immediately decided to investigate my beaded belt, even though it had to bend its head to do so(!), I started in Jizania's face.

And she smiled her carved little smile that I recalled so well.

"Good evening, Madam," I said.

"No, Claidi," she answered sweetly, "we don't use titles like that here anymore. Now I am only Jizania."

Only!

Then her amber eyes slowly left me and went to the man at my side. "And this must be the extraordinary Argul, leader-king of the Horse People, and adventurer-prince of the Wolf Tower."

Argul didn't bat an eyelid.

He looked at her and nodded. "Charmed to meet you," he said. "I think you're acquainted with my grandmother."

"Ironel? Oh yes. Many long years ago."

"Not so long," he said, friendly, "since I think she some-how contacted you recently, and told you a few things."

"Such as your true identity," said Jizania.

"That's the one."

The lion was now eating my belt. "Oh, stop that!" I snapped, giving it a push.

The lion growled, but only sullenly. It swung away and moved off.

"Of course," said Jizania, "Claidi has now no need to be afraid of a lion."

She knew about my ring. Knew about everything. Every-thing?? (It doesn't have to be that Ironel told her, either—could be Twilight!)

The indigo bird half-raised its wings. It wasn't as comfy as she with lions.

"Come along," said Jizania, "let's take our places. You'll sit with me, won't you, though I'm only an old woman and you are the guests of honor."

Argul gallantly offered her his arm. She liked this; her eyes sparkled a moment. He was prepared to flirt also with her. I remembered how she'd liked Nemian, too. Ironel was just the same.

He gave his other arm to me.

As we walked, I still had a silly, nasty sensation, recalling Nemian and Ironel that time in the Tower. The sort of *private party* they had going on between them. This wasn't that. Argul was playing clever. Though never forget, Claidi, your marvelous husband, too, is, as she reminded us, Wolf Tower blood.

Jizania sat down in a carved chair at the head of a table, with Argul on her left and me on her right. Dengwi sat at the other head of this table.

No one seemed concerned about the lions. As the Dinner started, people kept throwing them food. Maybe that was what stopped them pouncing on us and having *us* for dinner.

There were tons of food. What did we eat? Can't remember. Only what Jizania had.

She only ever had Teas. I'd learned that ages ago. And now, even though she was no longer a capital letters Old Lady, and we were celebrating the Night of Freedom, she was brought a whole separate set of dishes. There were tiny sandwiches, and marzipan fruits, and chocolate-bread, and a silky blancmange. There was even a teapot. And this silver plate piled up with tiny beans made of colored sugar.

"How little you eat, Claidi," she said amusedly to me. "I recall how little appetite you had last time."

Yes, I thought, I was nervous then, too.

I said, "But you eat even less." I couldn't somehow *bring* myself to call her by her name.

"I eat little, I need little. Not like Corris and Armingat

over there. Dear, dear. It's my interest in life that feeds me."

She offered her bird a buttered biscuit.

Then she started chatting—I mean *chatting*—to Argul. They talked all about Ironel and the Towers City, and the Hulta. I noted he was being careful, even though he seemed not to be, and also that no one yet had mentioned the north, or Ravens, or Twilight Star.

Jizania had conned me into taking the place of Twilight's daughter in the Wolf Tower. Though I couldn't read Jizania's mind, I *knew* she was still up to something. It wasn't just life she fed on, it was making things happen.

And then, something did happen!

The former lords and ladies were all sitting down with everybody else. (Flindel was particularly expert at lobbing roast to the lions.) Everyone also got up now and then to help serve each other things.

There was a young woman who served only Jizania. She, this woman, didn't sit down like the others. She sort of hovered and retreated. Jizania didn't speak to her. Jizania treated her—like a *slave*.

What with one thing and all the other things, I hadn't paid this person much—any—attention. I think I'd vaguely seen she had a flushed, screwed-up face—the only agitated girl present, apart from me.

She had no hair. I'd thought, I now think, this was because she seemed to belong to bald Jizania. (Though none of her maids had ever been made bald in the past.)

A man had just got to his feet to propose another toast we had to drink.

"Here's to our three Lion Night Heroines," he cried over the waterfall rush. He had been one of the kitchen slaves. "Fabulous Dengwi and Jizania and Claidi. Without them—none of this!"

Everyone stood up, but for the toasted ones, Jizania, Dengwi and me. As the glasses and cups were raised, Dengwi and I looked at each other. She shrugged.

But before I could either like that, or wonder what it *really* meant—

"Heroines—damn them!" screeched a high, unmusical voice just above my right ear.

Something held up next rattled down all over me. And I thought, Can't be very lethal, or the ring would have stopped it—but it—they—*are* sticky—

And then Argul was there and he'd thrust someone away and she had gone sprawling. And there she lay, this sprawled someone, honking: "I'd kill the lot of them! Kill all of you! Whipping—that's what you deserve—you scum—you *ants*—" And then a string of truly unwritable dirty words that, I'm embarrassed to say, I now know all the meanings of.

I stared at the writhing female earthquake on the terrace.

"It's Jade Leaf."

She'd finished (for now?) cursing us all. She sat there panting, rubbing a bruise on her arm where she'd fallen.

How could I ever not have known, even for a moment, that horrible squinched pointy face.

Even bald. (Why was she bald?)

"Why is she bald?" I said blankly to Jizania.

"She lost her hair," Jizania answered.

"*Lost* it?"

"It fell out." Jizania rose. She glanced at JL, that was all, but there was something unnerving in her glance. A sugar-bean dropped from Jizania's sleeve. I'd thought they were all down my neck.

"Er—" I said, "why is she—"

"Why did she stay?" Jizania arched her brows. "Her mother, when she left, didn't want her. And Jade Leaf was too afraid to go on her own. I allowed her to wait on me. She was no good for anything else."

"But I thought no one was to be a servant anymore—" I heard myself blurt.

"Come, Claidi. Are you protesting ill treatment of this pimple, who made your life a misery all the years you lived at the House?"

Well—was I?

Didn't know.

I'd always hated and feared Jade Leaf. Now she'd just thrown a dish of sugar-beans at me, and I thought . . . what?

A couple of people walked across to Jade Leaf. One of them laughed and poured a jug of wine or something all over her, over her shocking-pink face and unattractive frock and bald head where she'd lost her hair, perhaps from fright and unhappiness.

But anyway, she was angry now (I expected the liquid from the jug to sizzle) and no sooner had he done that than she scrambled up and went for him, so the other one pulled her off. *He* was just going to hit her really hard when Argul stopped him.

Then she balanced there, shivering with meanness and spite and helplessness.

She wouldn't look at any of us now.

In the past, she'd often had "tantrums." But given the position she was now in—

She's brave.

Stupid and rotten—but brave.

And Shimra, her mother, just left her.

And I can see Jizania has some (secret) special reason for making JL suffer. And that can have nothing to do with getting back at JL for me or for any other former maid.

Dengwi stood beside me. I hadn't seen her come up. Jizania had floated away.

"She's remembering that now Jizania will punish her in the morning," Dengwi said.

I felt a bit sick. Shook myself. I mean, JL had been no close friend of mine.

And had Dengwi?

"You approve of that?"

She didn't reply.

Jade Leaf was turning. She walked off the terrace and down into the Garden, and no one stopped her.

Then Jizania was calling us, Dengwi and me, back to the table. Her voice was kind, fond—like a mother's.

Then she called the tables to order. "Now *I* will propose a toast, if an old lady may be so bold."

Actually, she made a little speech.

It was very short. It said a lot.

I still haven't worked out what she's up to. Will I ever? Sitting here now in the warm clear light of Yinyay's library, I rack my brains. Have no answers.

I do know this. Jizania is more dangerous than any of them, than Ironel—even Twilight. She plays soft, like a lion's paw, but the claws are there inside. Then she plays sharp like the claws, but beware the softness!

As she told me, she feeds off life. Like the free lions with the meat.

Everyone else had sat down, and kept quiet at her invitation. So much for powerless old royal ladies. She pitched her voice easily over the noise of the waterfall.

"I am not your heroine," began Jizania modestly. "Claidi and Dengwi are the heroines." (Cheers.) (I was too uncomfortable now even to feel uncomfortable.)

"And all the more your heroines," announced Jizania, "because both these girls had more at stake than any of you have ever known." She raised her glass of pale tea. She said, "Claidi was not even a servant, she was a slave, born to a slave mother and a father unknown—for as you well recollect, a male slave's name was never noted, when a child was permitted him, only the slave-woman mother's."

Had she never told them this about me before? She had *always* known.

Jizania said, "But Dengwi triumphed another way. For though Dengwi's mother was a slave of the House, Dengwi's father was a prince. Prince Lorio. He isn't here with us tonight. He left us with the others. Only Dengwi is here. I raise my glass to Dengwi, then, a princess after all, and to Claidi, a slave now free."

There was a kind of spluttering nothingness in which about three slow-witted people still started to cheer, and then realized cheers weren't it anymore.

Somewhere someone dropped a cup. Even over the noise of the water, it was loud, this smashing sound.

Jizania sat down smiling. Old and wise and kind.

It was Dengwi who, back in her place at the table's opposite head, got to her feet.

She spoke as clearly as Jizania.

"Is this true?"

"True?" Jizania, a little vague now, a little, forgetful old lady. "What, my dear?"

"That my father was a *prince*." Dengwi's words came like bites into the darkness, left little holes.

"Oh yes. Lorio. He was briefly attentive to your mother. He even told her what name to give you."

I remember Prince Lorio, too. Everyone would. Ebony skin and iron eyes and two small bits of ice for mind and heart. He had been one of the monsters, here.

Dengwi's father—

And she could never have known.

I thought how Jizania had shocked me when she told me I was royal. At least that had been in private. (And wasn't true.) Nor had it been destructive.

But royalty was garbage at the House now. And so Dengwi, the Heroine, was now garbage?

Jizania had lied about me. This too might be a lie.

[69]

I got up, in the second Dengwi walked briskly away from the tables.

There was so much confusion all around now, mounting gradually into noise and argument, no one took any notice of me as I hurried after Dengwi, and Argul strode after me.

As for Jizania, eyes hooded, gentle as a poisonous snake that sleeps, she sat there giving another biscuit to the bird.

"Wait—Dengwi!"

Dengwi waited. There under the black velvet trees.

I waved at Argul, and he stayed where he was, so I could talk to her alone.

"She's a liar, Dengwi. She lied to *me*. I can tell you—"

"I don't think she's lying."

"She's made you trust her."

"Not really," said Dengwi flatly. "I just never expected—that."

"Why don't you think she lied?"

"Oh, I didn't know about this. It's just that I did know my mother awhile, before they let me be a maid instead of a slave. And Mum—she said to me I was being allowed a better position because of my father. So I said why, who was he? And she said she couldn't say, she wasn't allowed to say. I thought afterwards," said Dengwi, "she was making that up. Kidding herself that my dad had been someone royal. She was only young, my mother. About my age now. She only lived a few more years. Slaves don't—didn't—last."

We were walking slowly on into the black silence of the

trees. No one was near now. Only Argul, back there, burning like a distant lamp.

"She must have been proud," said Dengwi, "in a horrible way, that she'd been *honored* by a prince. But naturally I am ashamed of it. And now I'm an outcast."

"No, Dengwi, they wouldn't—"

"What did we rebel against?" she asked me. "Against the royalty. What am I half of? Royalty, it seems."

"Yes, but some of *them* have stayed."

"And you see how they are. Tolerated—and left on their own most of the time. Or picked on and driven mad like Jade Leaf. All but Jizania, who is—Jizania, and not like anyone else."

"Look, they won't turn against *you.*"

"Maybe if he'd been some other prince, someone halfway all right. But *Lorio?*"

We stopped walking and talking. We stood and looked at the darkness all around.

Finally she said, "I don't want to be his daughter, Claidi. I don't want that blood in me."

"No."

"And I don't want my own kind trying to pretend I'm just fine. Or having to keep with the other kind, like Flindel and Kerp—who might rather like me, now." She shuddered.

She didn't say, uselessly, *Why did she do this to me? Why did I ever trust her?*

Dengwi doesn't often waste words.

"What will you do?" I eventually asked.

"Leave."

"Where will you—?"

"Somewhere."

"Dengwi," I said, "Argul and I really came here to rescue you—"

And just then, over her shoulder, I saw something that took the rest of the sentence out of my mouth.

Down deep among the black trees had appeared two glimmering straight shapes, two coin-colored ghost faces, and two metallic round hats, like haloes—

At my start, Dengwi spun to look, too, and in that moment the figures flickered out among the shadows.

"Did you see—?" I said.

She hadn't.

And then the next second this other thing happened, because obviously so far the evening had been uneventful.

What it actually was, was Jade Leaf springing against us, giving a long, shrill shriek, with one of the fancy Dinner knives in her fist ready to plunge into our backs.

Luck was with us. It was me she struck first. She'd always disliked me most.

And of course, the ring—

There was a rush of light, like lightning, which shattered in flakes, and Jade Leaf was flung head first into a thicket about twenty feet away.

Dengwi looked me over.

"I have something that protects me," I said.

"So I see."

"We'd better go and look to see if she's hurt," I squeamishly muttered.

"I can hear her moving, I think."

We went to the thicket and peered in. Then we forced a way through and poked about. There wasn't a trace of her.

By then Argul was there. He looked, too. Nothing.

"She must have run off."

It did seem rather unlikely. After the way the ring had thrown her, you'd expect anyone to be stunned at least. But she wasn't there.

Across the trees we could hear shouting now from the terrace. It didn't sound very friendly. I thought of the first Lion Night, the roars and torches, the hunting down and driving out of royalty, and only not killing them because that was what the royalty themselves had been expected to do—

"Dengwi," said Argul, "you probably don't want to trust anyone right now. I'm going to ask you to trust the two of us. Give me your hand. Claidi, take her other hand."

She is sensible, even like this. I would have dithered, of course, resisting, quacking, *Why, what for?*

She just gave us her hands.

"Hold tight," he said.

She held tight.

And up we went, the three of us, into the night.

TO THE SOUTH?

Each of us saw the hot air balloon, too, as we crested the trees.

Didn't I say it had been a slow evening?

The balloon was a ways off, and seemed to be moving east to south, judging from where the moon was.

Moonlight reflected in a silver crescent around the balloon itself, and half-lit the basket thing below, but also, in the dark, fire from the thing that makes a balloon work shone up red on its underside. It looked unearthly, and menacing.

We'd dropped back a little, into the treetops.

From up here, not only could we see the balloon sailing slowly over, but also the crowd below on the big terrace.

"The balloon's why they're shouting."

There was panic down there. Lights flaring, going out. Some people were running away into the cover of the trees while others stood there, gawping upward, turned to stone.

Daisy's ghastly Jovis had stayed at the House—would he, and any other remaining Guards, now unpack the cannons and try to shoot the balloon down?

That didn't happen. Instead, the crowd left on the terrace grew quiet. And the silent, silvery-fiery thing went drifting on, and away, getting smaller.

"Whose is it?" I worried.

"Could be from anywhere," Argul said. "A lot of places claim to have them."

But the only place I'd ever found that did was the City of Towers. Which was south, where the balloon seemed to be going.

"Come on," he said.

And we lifted off again and sky-ran through the air, unseen by anyone on the ground, or (hopefully) in the balloon.

By the time we'd flown out from the Garden walls and into the desert, the balloon had grown as tiny behind us as a pea.

Yinyay was standing firm where we'd left her. She didn't seem aware of any threat.

We flew toward her big shape, Dengwi held really very easily between us.

She hadn't said anything. Well, all this must be sort of a surprise.

Maybe the House will end up capturing the balloon tonight, as one more sign of the rightness of Lion Night. It was Nemian's balloon that started everything. All this . . .

Perhaps this balloon was a coincidence.

And the masked statues I thought I'd seen—just a trick of the shadows?

Anyway, it had all been so dull so far, hadn't it; we were now ready for some excitement.

No sooner had we gotten into the downstairs foyer of Yinyay, and were standing on the marble (if it is) floor, with Dengwi gazing speechlessly up at the soaring galleries and stairs and lift-spaces, than Yinyay spoke.

"Welcome on your return," she said. "A letter has come for you, Claidi and Argul."

I'm writing this up now, as I said, in the library. (Thu is lying under the table snoring, worn out by some of the clockwork chase-fetch games Yin has made for him, and which he plays ceaselessly when we're not there, judging by the upended chairs!)

Dengwi's gone to a bedroom Yinyay arranged.

D still hasn't said much, and I'm concerned that she really is shocked, but she seemed calm, and Yinyay will keep an eye on her. (We did explain a bit about Yinyay, and the flying and all that, but it's too much all at once, isn't it.)

Can she trust us?—well, she has. Only because she felt she had to? And—can we trust *her*? (It's occurred to me how unlikely it would have been for the royalty to kill all their servants just because of my escape with Nemian. So saying they would was whose plan? Only Jizania's?)

And now, this other thing.

This letter.

You see, it's a "flying letter"—like the ones Venn was sent at the Rise. Yinyay can receive them, too. And I don't, never have, understand/stood how this works. But there it was and here it is, in front of me now.

After he read it, Argul said, "Leave all this for the morning."

But I'm on edge.

(I'd never told him about the statues from the grove, kept forgetting. I'll have to do that tomorrow, too. Then I can tell him how I may have seen two of them again tonight.)

Meanwhile, I'll copy the letter down here, I think. Oh, you'll know who it's from, perhaps, the way I did, the minute you see how it begins.

My dear Claidissa and Argul, I hope this finds you well.

Really, it's just like her other letter. And her curling, looped and ornamented writing, with something spiky and *hard* at its center.

Ironel.

(But why is she calling me Claidissa now? How can she know we're in Yinyay and *not* know I am *not* Claidissa, but only slave-born Claidi? Perhaps it's just her being awkward.)

"My dear Claidissa and Argul, I hope this finds you well. I, of course, am never well." (Hah! She's as fit as an alligator.) . . . "But I will not try your patience with my personal difficulties. I understand that your ventures have been a success. But now I have urgent news which you would be most foolish to ignore, and which, though it will astound you both, I am unwilling to put down here. Therefore, come to my private house, which your Tower-ship will find with no trouble, seven miles outside the City. Make haste; let nothing delay you. Remember, I have been your friend in the past."

And then her name, ropes of coils and swirls, as if she's trying to grow a hedge of thorns round it to hide her and what she really is.

And *then*, one of her little additions. This one quite astounding itself, in its way: "Make sure Dengwi comes with you."

"Do we go there?" I said to Argul this morning.

He frowned. "You think it's a plot."

"Why not? Seven miles from the City—which means seven miles near the Wolf Tower."

"At least it's seven miles."

"When we trusted her before it was only because we had to."

"And that worked," he said.

"You *do* think we should go."

He's her grandson. Ustareth was her daughter.

I thought of flying south, back to that grey River called Wide, that repellent City of stone. That Tower with a black stone wolf crouched on it.

"I've been to her house before," Argul reminded me, "and escaped alive. You know, I think I do want to know what this is about."

He looks—the same way I remember at Peshamba. As if he's thinking of other things, things that have been lost. Is it the idea of Ironel?

We agree to go south.

We go and tell Dengwi, who simply nods. She doesn't care about this, doesn't really want to talk to us, just to be by herself and think through what bloody Jizania's landed her with.

I didn't say Ironel mentioned her.

At least Thu is pleased we're off somewhere again. He's racing up and down and everywhere. Yin is moving at her top speed, but though you can slightly feel it, it's not uncomfortable. (The horses are fine.)

The ground is invisible, a blur. Yinyay says, like this, it will take less than a day to get there.

Oh, yippee. Back to the Wolf Tower and Ironel in less than a day!

THE HOUSE IN THE LAKE

He had told me, her mansion loomed over a lake. When we got there, the house was in the water. I was puzzled. Argul said, "There's been a flood."

It turns out that the lake (like Wide River and the marshes) is tidal. The tides had grown strong and run up over the flattish dry meadows, and stayed there. Only the first story of Ironel's mansion is under water.

And it was raining, anyway. I always remember it raining, or drizzling, at the City. Just once did the City sun come out— the day I left.

Yinyay had slowed down, coming in over some low, rocky hills, and I'd immediately gone to several windows, checking to be sure I couldn't see the WT anywhere. But I couldn't. It and the City really were miles off.

The mansion is greyish-yellowish, like the lake, and the sky.

Yinyay parked about a hundred yards away.

We'd discussed whether to have her shrink, but it had seemed safer to leave her outside and large, with the horses and Thu inside.

Then Thu made a scene because we were going out again without him. He yelled and jumped at us.

"We'll take him," said Argul. "Why not?"

"Because—of *her* is why not."

Argul looked exasperated. "Claidi, let's give the old woman the benefit of the doubt this once. And if anything goes wrong, Thu is a big, tough, canny boy."

I was uneasy. Always am where Ironel is involved. But Argul, it seems, isn't much. There's the difference.

Then there was Dengwi. Why should she want to come and see Ironel? She wouldn't. And if I told her about Ironel inviting her, she'd want to even less.

But Argul spoke to Dengwi, telling her quite a lot quickly and clearly. (I do admire people who can do that. Perhaps it comes from having been a Hulta leader.)

Dengwi nodded. She said, "Why does she want to see me?"

"We don't know. We don't know why she wants to see us. She's a mischief-maker. But I've found her helpful."

I said, "You don't have to go with us, Dengwi."

"No, of course not," said Argul. "You can just hang around here. Unless you're curious."

I saw Dengwi thinking about hanging around in (peculiar automatic) Yinyay, quite alone, wondering what the hell was going on in the mansion.

I saw that Argul had made her do this, and decide coming with us would be better.

More leaderly gifts, persuading people to do what they don't want to, while thinking it was their idea . . . ?

Is that so good?

Anyway, we all went.

We walked down to the shore of the lake, or the brink of the flood.

"We'll need to fly over," I said. "She must have known that. Perhaps it's another test, to see if we really can."

"She already knows *I* can. *She* gave me the Power sapphire," he said.

"Me then. Testing *me*."

Argul said, "Look."

I looked. A long grey boat was coming, rowed through the water, so folding glass ripples crawled away and away.

It reached us in five minutes. Inside was a grey oldish man and two younger grey rowers, to match everything else.

"Good evening, sir," said the older grey man, who is her steward here. "A pleasure to see you again."

And, like the prince he actually is, Argul nodded graciously, and shook the man's hand. "This is Ert," Argul introduced him. And us: "The ladies Dengwi and Claidi."

Both Dengwi and I bristled.

"Madam," said Ert to me. "Madam," he said to Dengwi.

"Neither she nor I," I said, "is a Lady Anything. Just call us Dengwi and Claidi, please."

But he never does. We both stay firmly "madam." And Argul stays *sir*. (Which is why, Argul says, he doesn't bother to keep telling Ert not to, anymore.)

Anyhow, just then, Thu eagerly jumped in the boat, nearly knocking Ert and the rowers into the lake. Perhaps the boat smelled of fish or something.

There aren't any elevators in her house. There are flights of marble stairs. And on each staircase, at one side or sometimes in the very middle, is a sort of rail, and down this comes suddenly whizzing, appallingly fast, a kind of throne.

That's how she appeared to us.

We were standing in the room we'd been taken to, looking at the stairs, and then the rail hummed, and next down the rail tore the throne at nine hundred miles an hour. It was made of gold-plated wood (they all are) and in it sat Ironel, grinning at us, as she rushed nearer and nearer.

That grin. Her teeth were no longer the pearl teeth Ustareth made her that she couldn't eat with. No, they were proper false teeth, looking very real, and well able to deal with food, as I saw later.

(Both these astonishments Argul apparently saw before, but never mentioned to me. He said, "I didn't think you'd want to know."

"But you said you'd seen the *pearl* teeth," I complained.

"Well, yeah, I did. They're for public display, or making

[83]

some sort of point. And she also wears them because of Ustareth. That's all.") All of this was said later.

Right then, the throne landed in the room and came to a halt. Ironel stood up and walked over to us.

She used to look tall. She doesn't now. Have I grown taller? Perhaps; Argul has. Her scranched-back iron hairstyle and her hard paper face, they were the same. Only they too looked smaller.

The black cane going tap-tap on the floor was unchanged.

"Madam," said Argul. And then, shocking me despite everything, "Grandmother."

It was what Nemian had said. Both Nemian—and Argul—have a right to say it. She *is* "Grandmother."

Only it made me go cold.

But, she'd helped us. Even me she had helped, or so it had seemed.

"Argul," she said. Him first, of course. "And are you still calling yourself that? Still Argul? Not altered your name yet to something more suitable and princely? I made a list for you, splendid ancient names from the Towers. You might like to glance at it sometime. Choose one."

He laughed.

She didn't mind. She likes *him* not being scared of her, anyway.

"Grandmother," said Argul, "I like my own name."

"Well, well," she said.

Then she gave him her hand to kiss and he took no notice and put his arm around her and kissed her cheek. (What does *that* feel like, I wonder? Toughened parchment? *Cement?*) She enjoyed all that, too.

[84]

Oh, he knows how to handle her.

But then, just because he can, it doesn't mean Argul (my Argul) is two-faced, like every other man and woman of the Towers.

Thu was quite genuine, anyhow. He hadn't been keen on the throne-rail; he didn't care for Ironel. He'd walked back, and now stood by me, growling softly.

So then Ironel saw me.

"Ah. Claidi." She seems to see that I want my own name, too, despite her letter.

"Madam," I said. That was all.

"Something's upsetting your dog," she said.

"You, madam." Too late. I'd said it.

"*I?*" She cackled her cackle. "*I?*" Ironel cranked her head around. "And this is Lorio's daughter."

I couldn't even look at Dengwi. I felt what happened to her face, her expression.

Something clicked home in my brain.

"So you do know," I said, "what Jizania told everyone last night."

"I do know, since Jizania was told to say it, and I was told she *would* say it."

I heard Dengwi catch her breath. Before I could shout *Told by WHOM?* Dengwi said, "Madam, are you saying it isn't true?"

Ironel looked Dengwi up and down. "How should I know? I have nothing to do now with your House-in-Garden. But I've seen a picture of Lorio. You have a look of him."

✦ ✦ ✦

OF COURSE she said absolutely NOTHING about why we were there.

We ate dinner in a big cold room that looked out over the dismal lake, as night came down and thankfully hid everything.

It was to be the first of several such grisly meals, full of foul food and talk about everything but her summons.

(By now I know why Ironel kept us waiting. But it doesn't improve things much.)

The first meal was tasteless; later ones would have the tastes of all the wrong things—too salty, too sour or sweet. And the whole house smelled of damp and mud. The high spot of that first evening's entertainment was when she took us to look down a spiral stairway into the lower story, at the flooded rooms shining faintly in lamplight from above. Now and then some big, vicious-looking black fish would shoot out of the water, then spear-thrust down again. They had teeth, too. (Thu brightened up, but sulked when I dragged him away.)

Argul and Ironel did talk. He told her things about the Hulta, Peshamba, and other places. Not the north. They didn't discuss the City or Towers much either. Never mentioned the Law. That was all settled, it seemed. (???)

He didn't say *anything* about her summons to us, and nor did I, until she said that now she was going to rest, and Ert would show us our rooms when we were ready. Then I said, trying to be Social, like Argul, "We'll sleep better if we know what you wanted to tell us."

"I doubt it," she rejoined.

"Why didn't you try to get it out of her?" I cried, when Argul and I were in our extra-icy bedroom, lovely with drafts, and either mice or fish rummaging around behind the walls.

"Why do you think?"

"She wouldn't have told us."

"Right."

"But she hasn't told us *anything*."

"And she still hasn't after you asked her."

"She'd have told *you*."

"She will tell me. In her own time."

"But—"

"Why," he said, "are you in a hurry to know?"

"Aren't you?"

"Like she said," he answered quietly, "maybe we're happier not knowing."

"Then why did we come here?"

He didn't reply. Oh, of course we had to come here and find out, and of course we didn't want to, not either of us.

As if we already knew. As if someone had whispered it to us when we lay asleep.

The others arrived two days and two nights after this.

It was raining, but I'd gone out for a walk with Thu. No one had mentioned that I might fly to the shore, my ring supporting both Thu and me. The boat was produced at once. And when I got out, and hauled the dog out—he just *loved* this boat!—it waited there at the flood-side for us to come back.

I stalked over the unpretty landscape, holding up an umbrella, while Thu bounded in all directions at once, or so it looked. The open country called—*he* didn't mind how desolate it looked. It was a *racetrack*.

Argul and I—we hadn't talked properly. He had seemed very shut-in again. This was beginning to remind me, against my will, of Venn. Venn's silences, his brooding and bad temper. Argul didn't get angry. But I'd never—had I?—felt this shutting-out before. Not before Peshamba.

He guesses, I thought, what we're going to be told, this news we have to wait for. But he hasn't told me what he thinks it is.

As for Dengwi, she'd shut herself up in the room Ironel gave her. When I looked in, D was always sewing things, or else doing complex, impossible-looking exercises on the floor. Bending her body into a backward hoop, standing and walking on her hands—I'd been all admiration, but then I saw that she just wanted me to go.

So I was alone up on a slope, looking down toward the lake, when I saw the carriage bumping along.

It had come out of a gap between two other highish slopes, across the lake. In the misty sludge light, I couldn't make out much about it.

"Thu!" I yelled. He barked. It was his "in a minute" bark. "No, Thu. *Now!*"

I felt I ought to get back to the house. Because in all this forlorn emptiness, where else could that carriage be going?

They pulled up by the lake and the boat, now with us in it, rowed over to fetch them. It was a round, dark carriage with huge wheels, and drawn by four enormous, ungainly birds, harnessed two by two. They had black bodies and pinkish-white necks, and long pinkish legs, and weaving heads all beak and irritation. They looked bottom-heavy, as if water had been poured down the necks and collected in the bodies, unable to reach anywhere else.

"What are they?" I asked Ert. Despite calling me madam, or Lady Claidi, he seems all right.

"Ostriches, madam."

I've heard of ostriches, I think. Didn't know they were quite so—unusual. (But they can certainly run fast—the carriage had rattled along.)

Thu growled.

"Shut up, Thu. They're ostriches."

Then the carriage door opened. The ostrich-driver(?) went round and put a step thing against the doorway, and now two people got out and walked over to the waiting boat.

"God, I've strained my back, I knew I would," the young man lamented. "Bloody carriage." He glared at the ostriches and the ostrich-driver, but disdained to comment further. The wonderful young woman at his side said nothing.

Then he glanced over at us.

"Oh, Ert, isn't it? The boat's a bit crowded. Did you need to bring all these people—and that dog—my wife's got her cat, you know, we don't need a fight on the lake."

I caught Thu's collar.

"Yes," drawled the man to me, "keep hold of it."

Thu actually was fairly relaxed. Perhaps cats bother him less than fish?

No, I was the one now who was unsettled and might begin growling.

He remembered Ert, but not me. No, not even after everything he'd done to try and ruin my life. The lies and betrayals, the sheer nasty petty nasty *pettiness*—

It was Nemian.

And the woman, exquisite Moon Silk.

They got into the boat. Nemian sat as far off as he could from Thu—or me. She said nothing.

He was wearing a coat of the richest black fur (just knew it wasn't fake) and black, black trousers and boots with designs sort of carved in them. And this velvet shirt, blue as the sky here never is, with streaks of satin somehow run through it. She was in white, again, this time with small polished stars fallen from heaven and scattered over all. Oh, her blue-ink hair, her flawless, primrose-cream skin, her graceful neck gracefully nestled by the slim grey cat with tilted violet eyes.

His hair is gold, still.

He's still an okk.

And she—well, she's like a beautifully bound book full of a few blank pages.

They said nothing to us, to each other, nor we to them, as the men rowed us across.

The entrance to the upper "dry" house stood open.

We got off at the balcony, which had become the improvised landing-stage.

"Flooded again," said Nemian in disapproval. He assisted Moon Silk onto the balcony, and they went inside. I followed, with Ert and Thu.

At the staircase that had the first whizzing throne, we waited. Obviously N and M knew the Ironel-Appearance Drill. Then he turned and looked at me. "Don't you have somewhere to be? Some duty to perform? You needn't stay to wait on my wife; she doesn't like strange servants."

I heard Ert's mouth opening, and put my hand on his arm. Yes, he *is* all right; he shut up. I said meekly, "Princess Ironel says I must."

"Well, I say you mustn't."

The total tronky beast. If I'd been a real servant here, what was I supposed to do now, risk Ironel's wrath or his?

I simpered. (Surprised he didn't remember me from that. I'm sure I must have simpered at him when I thought I had a thing for him. Dreadful thought.) "No, my lord. I really *must* stay."

"Now look here—"

Then came the noise of the throne-rail.

At once, Nemian forgot me.

He turned his handsome, useless head back toward the stair. And we all watched in suitable awe as Ironel rushed into view.

"Grandmother!"

Yes, it does remind me, that way he is with her, of someone confronting their personal goddess.

She rose from the seat and gave him her hand. He kissed it. At least he didn't kneel down this time; this wasn't a public occasion.

"Thank you for asking us over," said Nemian. "The City is so dreary these days." He added, "Your servant-woman there doesn't know her place, however. She insisted on disobeying me."

Ironel darted me a razor glance.

"That's true. She's an impertinent wretch. Which is why I like her."

Deflated, Nemian cast me his own look of Great Personal Annoyance. "You should punish her, Grandmother—"

"I should do as I wish. Enough. Let's go upstairs."

So she dismissed him. Were she and I in an alliance against Nemian? Doubtful.

She was back in the throne-seat and already speeding off up the stair, around a curve in the marble, and out of sight. *We* had to climb the stairs. Nemian droned on about having put his back out in the carriage. Ah, such a shame. Moon Silk just glided up. Thu and I stamped, an army of two.

At the top, we went into the gallery that overlooks the lake from floor-length windows. And there were Argul and Dengwi, looking out, already assembled, you might say.

Nemian swore when he saw Argul. Quite spectacularly. Argul, Nemian had apparently remembered.

Argul looked across at him, and his face registered very little, as it generally does when he's dealing with an enemy. Just the long look down his nose.

But Nemian blustered, "What is this barbarian oaf doing here in your house, Grandmother?"

And I rejoiced, because that meant Nemian still knew entirely nothing about *anything*.

I didn't even mind when she told him.

"He is neither. He, too, is my daughter's son."

"Alabaster only had one child—me!" squealed N, childishly.

("Yes, after you, once would be enough," remarked Argul mildly.)

"You forget," said Ironel, "my other daughter."

"Uzziyiff? *She was exiled*—"

Oh, he really didn't know a thing. Even her name.

"Exile did not prevent her," said Ironel, "from producing her second son."

Nemian flailed, mentally and physically. We all watched. Even Thu and the cat.

"No—*no*. If that's true—that would make him my—"

Nemian, really appalled. Quite a sight.

"Your cousin. You are correct."

"He's a bandit-barbarian. He's half horse and with the brains left in the horse's backside."

Argul moved across the floor so fast, so effortlessly, I think he partly used the Power sapphire to do it. But his reflexes are a fighter's; maybe it was only that.

He caught Nemian by the fur lapels and slapped him open-palmed across his face. Nemian reeled—it had looked more effective than any punch. When Argul let him go, he nearly fell over. Until Thu, who had decided to growl after all, now launched himself and landed smack on Nemian's velvet chest. Then Nemian did go over flat, and Thu stood on him, rumbling in his face. Nemian screamed for help.

We all stood there. And I thought, I never saw Argul get angry like that for something so stupid—now is he going to let Thu kill Nemian—do we definitely want that?

Argul said, "Thu. Off. Good boy."

Ironel had loved all this. *Loved* it.

Had I? I don't know.

Dengwi moved over to Thu and smoothed his head, and his hackles went down.

Nemian went on lying there, too scared, or stunned, surprised to get up.

"Shall we have tea?" twinkled Ironel.

And at that moment, exactly then, there was a terrific bang from above.

Everyone, even Nemian, goggled up at the ceiling.

It had sounded like a flying cow, or several flying pigs, landing on the roof, which over this gallery was flat.

"Princess," said Ert, "I'll go to see what's happened."

But he didn't have to.

What had happened was about to show itself to us.

At the long windows washed by falling rain, a flutter of darkness and brightness, like massive wings.

Then, through the glass we saw them, poised there in the air, staring in at us with enraged white or black faces framed by soaking wet, mud-splashed hair and clothes. The cursing one was Venn, and the shouting one was Ngarbo from Chylomba. It was Winter Raven, though, flaming mad, who kicked in the window with one blow of her furious boots.

US

Not every window will open for a Power jewel, it seems, not if the window doesn't open anyway, and the gallery ones don't. Naturally very aggravating, if you have been out in the rain for hours, and before that had been knocked about all over the sky by tempests and storms—not to mention a seasick balloon.

Yes, that balloon we'd seen was *them*.

But as so often before, I'm ahead of myself.

I must put all this next bit down very carefully.

I'd told her to go and see Venn at the Rise. I'd said, Winter, use your Power necklace and fly over the sea, the same as Ustareth did. Go and meet him—he's gorgeous.

She had always wanted Venn. She'd been supposed to marry Venn. Or Argul. All part of the Ustareth-Twilight plot to breed us all in correct pairs, and produce children even better than we were. (!)

And I had thought Winter would risk the journey—risk the sea flight, and meeting Venn.

She had.

This much, so far, she's told me. Flaunting, offhand: "You see, Claidi? I went and got him."

Venn doesn't look "gotten."

More *fetched*. They all do. They were.

Ngarbo, who insisted on accompanying Winter (he deeply fancies her—that was plain enough at Chylomba), told me the most about their journey to the Rise. But he didn't say much about when they got there. It must have been uncomfortable for Ngarbo. I don't know why he insisted on going along. Ngarbo always looks glorious, all in black, skin and (smart Chylomban) clothes, though not now in his uniform from the Raven Tower. It must be difficult for him, maybe, to grasp that Winter is intent on this other man. Venn really isn't quite as handsome as Ngarbo, nor a quarter as worldly wise, not trained to fight or even to *fly*. Ngarbo's led a full life, a lot of it spent as one of Winter's own personal soldiers. He even *says* he went with her out of "duty," as her bodyguard.

Anyway, when they *were* at the Rise—guess what. A flying letter came.

It arrived, not in Venn's room, either, but *fluttered out of the trunk of a tree* near where they were sitting.

Not all the Rise trees are simply trees, then. Like some of the animals—tiger-rabbit vrabburrs—and people—Jotto.

The letter was from Ironel. It was like the letter *we'd* had. Ngarbo said basically it told them that Ironel had urgent news she couldn't give on paper, but which would be *fatal* for them to ignore.

Winter, I gather, said, "Wolf Tower muck. So what?"

It was Venn who became slowly and desperately concerned. It was Venn, the one who once claimed to me that he preferred reading about things to doing them, who finally challenged Winter to find him a method of flying to the City and Ironel's house.

She agreed, because he was Venn. And Ngarbo agreed because *she* had. But I bet there was a row.

I began to see a pattern, though. Maybe you do, too. Argul and Venn, they were the two who felt compelled to find out what Ironel had to say, and were also so edgy.

Venn, in fact, now looked near to collapse.

Probably from the journey over here as much as anything.

Venn's Power ring hadn't worked, but it seems Winter was able to recharge it with a chip she'd cracked off the raven statue, which recharges the jewels at the Raven Tower. So off they all set.

Winter and Ngarbo had had fine weather on the way there. Their Power jewels just breezed them along. (I got the feeling they quite enjoyed it, being free of the Raven Tower and Twilight, and going somewhere new.) They even slept, as it were, on the wing, the jewels keeping them safe and on course. However, no sooner did they take off again from the coast, with Venn, than they ran into a storm.

("I thought we'd had it," said Ngarbo. "I know *you* did," spat Winter. Venn merely scowled.)

The jewels kept them in the air, and held each of them in a kind of protective envelope. But even so, the hurricane-type wind threw the *envelopes* around, so inside them the travelers were tossed head-over-heels or spun in circles.

In the end, Ngarbo said he spotted an island. They made for that and took shelter among falling palm trees and blown-over bamboos. When everything eased off, they went straight on.

They had some food with them—just as well, because there was no more land till they reached the coast. The sea went on and on, and then there was another storm.

Their general account of this was so angry and muddled—they kept interrupting each other with luridly sarcastic remarks. (Meanwhile, we were standing around in one of Ironel's big rooms, and Ert and others tried to serve us all tea.)

I think Winter must sharpen her tongue with a knife each night.

At last, they said, they made landfall, and then they didn't know where they were. Even if they were on the right *land-mass*—there are seemingly several.

"Then Venn had this idea," grated Winter, "of looking out for the places you'd written about so descriptively, Claidi. That was clever of him, wasn't it? *Such* a good thing he accidentally read all your diary that time."

I stayed blank.

Also, they told us, they found a town along the coast that had balloons. Worn out from flying in the storms, they bought a balloon and took off inland, and westward. And sure enough, in the end, Venn "recognized" the House in the desert.

"You went in very close. They might have used cannon on you," I said, "just as I so descriptively described in my *diary*."

"By that time," said Ngarbo, "I'd have *liked* them to."

It seems, having survived all the tumult in the air pockets, now Venn and Ngarbo got seasick in the balloon. Not *her*. Oh, of course not. She'd just stood there mocking them as they heaved over the sides, decorating the undeserving countryside far below.

"We had no ballooneer," said Winter. "Now *I* had to manage the thing alone. We followed your described route, Claidi. I did pretty well."

I glanced at Venn. He was gazing anywhere but at me, trying to drink a cup of tea and looking ill. Of course, too, trying to see anything or anyone but Argul.

"In the end," announced Winter crisply, reaching for a third cake, "the balloon was too slow, especially with these two throwing up morning, noon, and night. We ditched it, and did the rest under our own Power."

Presumably Ironel sent them instructions, too, on how to find her house.

Winter now strode over to Argul. She stood smiling at him a radiant smile which said, You *would never have been sick in a balloon*. You *would have been a dream*. Then she turned to Ironel. "We got a glimpse of your City on the way in," said Winter. "It's a dump, isn't it."

Ironel gave a yap of laughter. It was Nemian (who'd stayed quiet till then) who had to object.

"It's one of the finest cities on earth."

Winter flicked him a look. Somehow he seemed to recall that when she'd burst in, he'd been lying on the floor. Winter said, "How embarrassing that you should think so."

For a moment I watched him trying to work out if she had apologized to him or insulted him. But even that didn't cheer me up much.

They'd finished the story now. (I've added some details from my talk afterward with Ngarbo.) A stiff silence fell. In it could be heard the sound of Ironel's servants boarding up the shattered window.

"Sorry about that," said Winter unsorrily.

"Don't fret," said Ironel. "I'll get Twilight to take the cost out of your pocket money."

Winter flushed. "I don't see my mother now," she said, nail-hard. "We have a difference of opinion."

Then I saw that Venn was now looking right at Argul, and Argul looked back at him, unreadable.

Together like this, they don't look at all alike. Argul dark-skinned, his fall of hair so black, his assurance, so total. And Venn, fair skin tanned another shade by weather and pale from nausea, brown hair almost blond today, loosely curling on his shoulders, nervous, arrogant.

It was Venn, though, who moved forward. He put his tea-cup as he passed in someone's grasp, and went straight to Argul. Venn held out his hand. "I greet you belatedly, brother. How do you do?"

Argul shook the hand. He said, quietly, "Likewise."

And I thought, *He, too*—he, too—*is out of his depth in this.* Brothers—half-brothers—who've never met until now. Lives utterly unlike, couldn't be more so.

And her. Ustareth, that mother who left them both, Venn because she had been forced by the Towers to marry and have him, Argul because she had had to die. My heart—turned over. And over.

Then I realized that I was the one Venn had dumped his cup with, as if I were a table or something.

I put it down, and as if at a signal, Ironel spoke.

"Thank you, Ert. You and the others can go."

They went.

"I think," she said, "if everyone has had enough tea . . . Perhaps it's time I gave you your news."

She got to her feet. As she did so, I saw she leaned rather heavily on that cane of hers. And her wicked face—seemed aged under its oldness.

And in that moment I, too, Claidi, slowest of the slow, I too *knew*—

If I could, I would have stopped her.

But it was already too late.

"We will go into the next room," she said.

So we did. Muddy, windswept Ngarbo, Winter, and Venn. Nemian, now glaring at me, having realized who I am, and Moon Silk, serene in her personality-minus state. Argul and I. Dengwi, still the unknown quantity.

All of us.

✦ ✦ ✦

"I waited until you had all arrived. I did not wish to repeat this. To say it once will be enough."

Yes. It would have knocked her sideways. Of course it would. Any pleasure she got from knocking all of us sideways, too, might only be a slight compensation.

"I think some of you by now may—" she paused. "But why delay. It's soon said. My daughter, Ustareth Novendot Vulture-Ax of the Towers, is alive. She is alive and at work far to the south. Beyond the City. Across the sea.

"She told me," said Ironel, "and instructed me to tell each of you. I know very little of her plans for you. But she has plans. Not for all, it's true. Nemian, you and your wife . . . Moon Silk . . ." (she seemed to pretend not to recall the name for an instant; maybe she didn't) "you have only been told in order that my daughter Alabaster may also learn, and the Towers. I have no intention, myself, of carrying them this information. You will do it. You may add what is obvious. Ustareth has no fear of them, now. She's more powerful than any Tower, as perhaps you already believe."

She looked her old black-grey look at us.

As her eyes went over me, I shivered. But not because of Ironel—it was, that second, as if *Another* looked through her.

But Ironel was all I could look at. Like Venn now, I couldn't look at Argul. I couldn't look at Venn, either.

"The rest of you," she said, "you six young creatures." She smiled. "Ah, youth." Her voice was regretful, bitter. "You have it and think it will always stay. What I could do with that youth of yours, if *I* had it *now*. But it comes only once. And you waste it, don't you. Yet that, of course, is your right."

She said: "Ustareth invites you, her sons Venn and Argul, Claidis now called Winter, the daughter of Twilight Star, once Ustareth's friend, and also Claidi once called Claidissa, Dengwi, and Ngarbo—" (she had no trouble recalling *his* name; he's a man, and dreamy) "—who, though unrelated to her original plan, have come to her notice through their skill and wit, bravery and dash."

Are we supposed to be flattered?

In a way, a dreadful way—I sort of am. Sort of. Because this is Ustareth the Great talking here, through Ironel. Ustareth of the endless games and tests and heartless abandonments—but also the She bold enough to fight the Towers before anyone ever did, and clever enough to *win*.

But—oh, she left Argul, too. (Like Venn.) He was ten years old, and she lied and left him. Left his father, whom she'd said she loved. And the Hulta.

That's what she's really good at. *Leaving*.

No. I *won't* be flattered. No.

It was Dengwi who interrupted.

"Why have *I* been chosen?"

"I told you, girl." Ironel doesn't like interruptions.

"No. You haven't."

"You've been watched," said Ironel. "All of you have been watched. She watches everyone."

"Only a god," said Dengwi, "could do that."

(How does she know about God—I never did till I left the House, which never mentioned anything like that.)

I saw Venn give Dengwi a hard, angry look.

Ironel, too, impatient: "Your valor, Dengwi, on the night of the rebellion, was noted."

"And what Jizania told me? The other thing."

"Yes, that too. Jizania has taken her recent instructions from Ustareth. Why else were you cast out of your Garden and brought here?"

WHAT has Jizania told Dengwi? I mean, this other thing—

Ironel held up her hand in a wish-I-could-slap-you way. "Allow me to finish. I'm old, and this is tiresome. You are to use the transport which Argul and Claidi have been given and which will easily carry the six of you in comfort. You're to go south. Ustareth has sent to me a scientific code which can be added to Yinyay's mechanism. It will act like a route map. The journey will then be simple."

I wanted to say, *Why the hell should we go?*

But it wasn't *for* me to say, was it. I'm only someone else she's found interesting to spy on and mess with now and then. It is for Argul to say, and Venn. They're—Hers.

"What's in the south?" demanded Winter. "Apart from Ustareth."

"She has made a new land," said Ironel, "a country." Yes, I knew Ustareth could do that. She'd made the jungle-forests and the Rise, and the great Star-ship. A country—well, child's play.

"In that place," said Ironel, "she'll meet you. But be warned, the Powers you now have in such lavish amounts, your flight, your defenses—even the flying Tower of Yinyay—will lose their ability once you are on her borders."

My voice came out very clear. "Another game," I said.

Ironel speared me with her sad, cruel eyes. "What else is any of it? Yes, Claidi, you truly rid my City of the Law, and made it dull for my grandson Nemian. But there are other laws. Everything is subject to a law or a rule. How many will you break before you give up?"

And I heard myself say, "Every one I can."

She sighed. "You're young," she said.

Like small pebbles struck by a much larger stone, we've separated from each other. We wander about Ironel's mansion.

Nemian sulked because he's been formally recognized as Useless, and left out. He did try, despite her put-down, to flirt with Winter, who just said, "Go away." (In fact, she said something else, but that's what it meant.) So then he sulked about that, too. To me he wouldn't speak. One bright spot.

Venn also hasn't spoken to me.

Argul—Argul hasn't spoken to me.

I walked along here, to the spiral staircase, half-looking for Dengwi, but didn't find her. I am staring down at the murky lake in the bottom story. Thu is here, too, very happy to look at the (fishy) water.

I did meet Ngarbo. That was when he added the bits about the journey and the letter.

The weirdest thing was that I passed Moon Silk in a gallery, alone but for her cat. She was stroking the cat, which purred and looked beautiful. She was beautiful, too, but as I went by, she spoke to me. Hey, she can speak.

"Thank you for your kindness," she said.

!!!!!

I stopped. Why is nobody *ever* what you think?

"What kindness?"

"Long ago. Bringing him back to me."

"Oh. You mean Nemian."

"Yes. And for destroying the Law. You were very brave. The Law was so awful. I had always feared it. Now it's gone." (So, that at least is truly settled. I think.)

But she, too, looks sad. She's so beautiful and calm and—well, one-dimensional. You don't see that she's sad at first. Then you do.

He is such a heel, Nemian. He goes off with other women at the first chance. But he loved Moon Silk once. I remember he cried when he saw her again that first time. And she loves him, or why else did she thank me?

Poor Moon Silk. Poor all of us.

I know we'll be going south. Because how can Venn and Argul resist the magnetic pull of this wondrous/terrible vanishing/reappearing mother?

I just wrote that, and then—

Am I going mad? But Thu saw, too.

He thought it was a fish at first. (So did I.) A disturbance in the floodwater down there. And then we both jumped. Out of the depths, rising like a horrible waterlily, a tube of stone, a hat like a gold upside-down umbrella, a face that was a mask—

It was there—and then it sank, and was gone.

We are "watched." Are they, too, Her watchers? But more than that, *what* are they? And how have they followed me all the way here from Peshamba?

ROUGH CROSSING

I have called my horse Mirreen. It's a Hulta name, and a bit like *Sirree*, of course—that's why I chose it. Also something *I* could decide.

We've been fast sail-flying for some days. The coast is already behind us. Nothing much to say. (Didn't see the City of the foul Towers.)

Before we took off, Argul and I did talk. Of course we did.

We exercised the horses and Thu before we left Ironel's. After we'd ridden for about an hour around the lake, we took a breather. It was then.

And it was raining, naturally. It never stopped all the time we were there. But this was a faint, light rain.

I was trying so hard to—not to say anything, because *he* hadn't, not about any of THIS, and now I felt I'd burst. I meant to turn to him very reasonably and murmur, *I understand if you just can't talk about this—but, if you would like to, here I am. Perhaps we should.*

What came out was, "Argul, I've had enough of this. I can't stand it. Say something to me."

"Great weather," said Argul.

"No, I don't want jokes."

Then we dismounted, left the horses to browse the wet, thin grass, while Thu chased his own shadow.

We trudged slowly along a hill. Again, no one spoke.

Then he said, "It's awkward, Claidi."

"Yes, yes, I know it is. But—"

"I don't want to discuss it much."

"No."

"Somehow I knew, in a way. I knew since Peshamba. Half knew. I dreamed of her one night, I can't remember what. But it was Zeera—was Ustareth. And after that I felt—she was alive, but I couldn't see how."

We stopped. We gazed out as if admiring the divine view of all that sloshy nothing.

"Well," he said, "she just left us, my father and me. Like she left Venn."

"Yes."

"I have to get used to that. I saw her buried, Claidi."

"It must have been another of those lifelike dolls she's so good at making—like the one she left with Venn, that he and I found in the village in the jungle."

"No, it can't have been a doll. My father held her in his arms, I saw him, after she was—when she was dead. And I hugged her good-bye. I was ten. I know I was hugging *her*. She was real flesh and bone, Claidi. Just—dead."

Another long silence.

I said, "She's a manipulative witch."

He looked at me.

"All right. I won't argue with that."

"Sorry," I said. "I shouldn't have said that to you. It's just—her *games*—and this is only another new game."

"I have to find out," he said, "what it is."

I started to say something else, but he held up his hand. Then he turned and kissed me gently.

We walked down and mounted up again and rode for another hour or so.

That was it, really.

None of us was at the mansion for long after that.

Nemian and Moon Silk left in their ostrich carriage soon after Winter told Nemian to get lost. (I have wondered about the ostriches. Before I ran away from the City, having destroyed the Law, I'd passed a few laws myself. One had been to bring in animals and care for them. So were the ostriches—and M's cat—thanks to me?)

Apart from meals, the rest of us still kept pretty much apart.

Venn and Argul were *very* polite to each other. Venn and Dengwi were very *chilly* to each other. They really seemed to have taken a dislike to each other—why? (And I'd thought her so sensible and self-controlled.) I suppose we were all worked up.

To me, Venn still didn't speak (and still doesn't) beyond the unavoidable, like: "Oh, hello, Claidi."

I had one almost-conversation with Winter. She was lounging around, looking fabulous, brushing her short raven-black hair and painting her perfect mouth mauve in her milk-white face. She suggested that she and I go for a fly in the rain, "eh, Claid?" I'm afraid I replied, "In that lipstick? No thanks."

Perhaps I should have been nice, but she's so overpowering. Worse now, because she is demonstrating to everyone that Venn is her Conquest. But I think he isn't.

All this lasted only one day, and then we'd made up our minds—apparently (I mean *who* had? *I* hadn't), and we all went out to Yinyay. And then it was most of them trying to pretend as if Yinyay was just another house—or vehicle—and only Ngarbo admitting, "Quite a place," and Winter flying up and down *inside* Yinyay, throwing sticks and dog biscuits to Thu, nearly driving him nuts—

And now we are all up here together in the air. Wonderful.

Ironel didn't wave us off. She took to her bed. (Like last time in the Wolf Tower.) Ert told us she sent her regrets and good wishes.

Perhaps this time she did feel ill or upset. Of all of us, maybe, it was the worst for her, suddenly finding out that her long-lost genius *dead* daughter was alive a world away, across the vast southern sea.

✦ ✦ ✦

Venn spoke to me today.

How I wish he hadn't.

I was in Yinyay's library, and he strolled in, looking much better, and as always now, very elegantly dressed.

"The weather's improving," he said, "do you think so?"

"Yes," I said. Then, as that sounded a bit short, added, "I like your shirt."

I felt I ought to be friendly to him. We'd been friends. Kind of. Anyway, it was an error.

"Thanks," said Venn. "Well, here we are." Sitting on the table, swinging one long booted leg, looking dashing and irresistible.

"Winter not with you?" I asked.

"Winter is having Yinyay fit her for seven hundred elaborate garments."

So had he, I thought.

He said, "I gather you're responsible for landing me with her. Claidi, I ought to be angry with you."

"You ought to be thanking me," I said, "she's marvelous."

"Oh, she's all right to look at," he said. "But if I'd had any fond feelings for her, which I didn't, I'd have lost them during the balloon ride."

I thought, Ngarbo didn't. But then Ngarbo has known her probably since they were children. He makes allowances, or just doesn't care.

Venn gave me one of his swift, intense glances, so uncomfortably well remembered.

I had the uneasy, sudden idea that he now put on his best clothes, endlessly washed his hair . . . for me.

Was this self-centered of me?

"Claidi," said Venn, "you and Argul—you don't seem, how shall I put this, quite together."

He is no longer taller than Argul. They're the same height. Apart, Venn really does look so like him. But different.

"How are Treacle and Grem?" I asked brightly.

"Fine."

"They didn't mind your leaving?"

"There's much more going on at the Rise these days. Jotto keeps throwing parties. A real social swirl. The villagers come and go. Treacle's taken up with a boy who can grow thick striped fur all over himself."

"Like a vrabburr—"

"More like a badly upholstered wasp."

"You don't approve."

"Well. I didn't think he was good enough for her."

Then he is possessive of Treacle, too.

And still of me?

"If she's happy—"

"Are *you*?" he asked.

"Yes. If it's any of your business."

"Claidi, come on. It *is* my business."

"Why?" I unwisely said.

He told me.

"I don't give a damn about Winter Ridiculous Raven. And I didn't beg you to send me a replacement love interest, Claidi. You're the one who pushed into someone else's business."

"Yes. But she'll have told you why—"

"Winter and I were meant for each other? Tower rubbish.

For God's sake. It was you—" he broke off. He cleared his throat and said, staring earnestly at a large book on soapmaking, "It was you I—you were the one, Claidi. You still are. *You* are the reason why I came on this jaunt. Not for her—not either of those women—Winter, let alone *Ustareth*. You."

"I don't want to hear this."

"That is rather silly, isn't it," he said in a drawl, "you listened to it when I said it to you before. All right. You're with *him*. But has that worked, Claidi? Because if it hasn't—"

"Of course it's worked!" I shouted. "He's my husband, I'm his wife. If you spoke to Winter at all, *she'd* have told you how we were—and are."

"She did. She went on and on. The Peerless Partners, in two unmatched sets: You and Argul, her and me. But she isn't the one."

I got up and edged by, allowing a lot of room between us.

But he didn't try anything. He'd lowered his eyes.

Then, as I reached the door, it opened and Dengwi came in.

"Oh, charming," snarled Venn, looking violently at her. "This place is becoming like market day. It'll be standing room only soon."

The library is quite large. I thought, How many market days has he seen, he led such an isolated life at the Rise—

But Dengwi really surprised me, meeting his eyes in a long, cold, lit-up glare.

"I didn't know, *Prince*, that the library was exclusively yours. You should put a notice up."

"Yes. What would it say? *Keep out all unwanted bores.*"

"Er," I said.

But Dengwi said, "That would rather defeat your purpose, Lord Prince, since you yourself would be the least-wanted arch-bore."

It was like watching a ball game. I looked one way at her, then at him, then back at her, as they said some nasty and sometimes quite clever things to each other. But in the end I thought they wouldn't ever stop, so I made my getaway.

Later I said to her, "I know he was rude, but—" And she tossed her head like an angry horse and said, "He's not only rude, but royal all through. I can't stand his kind." And walked off (on her hands) before I could feebly defend him. I mean, he *is* a bit like that. He was pretty insufferable to me before he decided to like me. And I suppose she is extra sensitive to that, too, after the Lorio stuff.

Tonight at dinner, I wanted to ask *him* what he disliked so much about *Dengwi* (apart from the fact that perhaps he thought she interrupted before he could say something really devastating to me). But he sat there looking grim, and I thought he might take my question as me trying to resume our Talk. So I kept quiet. He did say something about Dengwi, though, loudly and the moment she walked in. "Here comes the Queen of bloody Night."

And off they went again.

Maybe it gives them something to do. And Ngarbo and Winter something to do, being the audience, though eventually Winter starts to look furious as well, since Venn was paying Dengwi all the attention, and Winter really likes a good argument herself. It's not my problem.

But I don't know what to do about Venn, I mean the way

he was with me. I feel sorry for him. And at the Rise—almost so much more . . . And he's probably desperate now about Ustareth. And—he spoke to me, and Argul—doesn't. So do I slap Venn, or try to be unromantic friends?

After they've really said good-bye, people should never have to say hello, again. There's a lesson there for *Ustareth*, too.

The bad weather is now only in here. Outside, the skies are blue. At dawn and sunset, gold and vermilion.

I can see this, as we've slowed right down. That made me afraid we were already approaching—*there*.

I braved it and asked Yinyay if U's scientific route map now tells Yin we're getting near.

And luckily Yinyay says it will take many days yet.

I'd said to Argul, one night when we were alone, and as usual not talking much, "Do you understand this thing about none of the Power jewels, or Yinyay, being any use when we reach this other country?"

"Perhaps."

When he didn't go on, I said abrasively, "She must have done it to *test* us all again." (I try hard not to say things like that, or that way to him, about *her*, but can't help it.)

Argul said, "It may not be that. Sometimes, if there's one very powerful force field, it can spoil any others."

"What's a force field?"

He did try to explain. I didn't get it really. (*She* had told him about them, of course.) They are areas of—well, *force*, created by machines. Something like that?

Yinyay no longer knows anything helpful about Ustareth.

(She can only find her now because Ustareth supplied the route—on a bead we had to feed into a tube Yinyay produced.) Her forgetfulness is Venn's fault, of course. He made Yin, the moment we found her in the jungle, wipe away all her knowledge of U, who had *made* her. Thanks again, Venn.

However, I went and asked Yinyay, now, if we were slowing down because of a force field. "Yes, Claidi," she softly replied.

We're not even in sight of this—*continent*, Yinyay calls it. And even so, its forcefulness is draining Yin's.

Yes, it is.

At dinner the food was cold and the wine had gritty bits in it.

Later, when Winter nearly went plunging to the marble below, doing one of her takeoffs from an upper gallery, Ngarbo sprang and caught her. They landed in a heap on the next gallery down, untidy but unhurt.

Then she tried to charge up her Power amber from the raven chip she brought with her. And it didn't do a thing.

We had a meeting and discussed this.

The discussion led nowhere except a shouting match. We were all involved but Argul. He just got up and walked out. I suppose I've seen him do that with the Hulta, with his men, when he didn't think it mattered. Why, though, doesn't he be "leader" and take charge of us all? Yes. He can't be bothered, can he.

After a while, I walked out, too. Dengwi followed me. From the look of things, I'd thought she'd have preferred to stay and provoke Venn.

But she said, "It's tough for you."

"Yes. For Argul it's worse, though. And for Venn."

She didn't frown. Just said, "They're both really this woman—Ustareth's—sons?"

"They are." I told her the facts quickly, and she listened. Then I said, testing her, "Didn't Jizania tell you about Ustareth?"

Dengwi hesitated. She said, "Not much. She didn't tell me that much, Claidi."

"Just a couple of things."

"That's right."

We walked on along the corridor, which, like all of them, has attractive panels of (what looks like) semiprecious stones set in the walls.

"Look," she said idly, "jade. In *leaves*."

"I wonder what happened—" I said.

"—To Jade Leaf?" we both finished.

Then we looked at each other.

Perhaps I shouldn't have, but I wanted to trust her again. I did once. And now I feel I can't quite trust—I don't know, anyone. I don't include Argul. Of course I trust Argul. I do.

"Dengwi, what else was it that Jizania told you, the thing that bound the two of you close together?"

She dropped her gaze. (Like Venn.)

"It wasn't exactly that *it* bound me to her," said Dengwi. "More that I felt bound to her because she'd told me."

"And?"

"Claidi—" She looked hard at me again. "It was something I believed, and now I don't know if I can, after the other thing—the stinking thing about Lorio being my father. I have to think, Claidi. It's what I've been trying to do. Until I can make up my mind if that first piece of information is true, I don't want to tell anyone. I don't want to tell you."

"I see. Right."

"You *don't* see; you think I'm being suspicious. What can I say. Give me time." Her eyes concentrated on me as they had that day at the House, when she said I mustn't be whipped. "I promise I will tell you, when I know in my own mind."

And with that I have to be satisfied.

And with all—*this*.

And the glory of the sunset furls away into the opening arms of night.

OLD MOTHER SHARK

Soon after the next day's sunrise, Yinyay dropped into the sea. Quite a splash. The last of her powers kept everyone, including Thu and the horses, unharmed. Not even a bruise. A lot got broken otherwise. I think Yin had to choose whether to lose things or lives, and luckily chose us.

This is like what happened last time, in the Star. The crash landing, and then—going it alone?

We sat in the rubble, really shaken up, all of us—you can imagine—as Yinyay bobbed, upright like a huge cork in the ocean.

We had been warned (*thank* you, Ustareth dear). But hadn't expected this so quickly, so completely.

Yinyay spoke to us.

Her tone was musical and quiet, but easily heard, as always.

Soon you couldn't hear her, though, for the noise of people yelling. Thu started to bark, too.

When all of that subsided, Yinyay had stopped—I mean her voice had apparently ceased working.

"Oh, well done," I said. "The last thing she could tell us, and you made sure we missed it."

"Claidi, always so well balanced," sneered Winter, "always patient, never raising her little voice—"

"Shut up!" I bawled.

Argul said, "I did hear the last part. Everything has stopped functioning. Nothing's wrong with Yinyay, but the edge of a greater Power source has rubbed out her own. The same with the Power jewels. They're dead. As Ironel already told us would happen."

They all began yowling and cursing again, all but us and Dengwi. But she'd never been given any Power jewelry to let her fly, or open doors, or prevent someone from stabbing her in the back. She hadn't gotten so she depended on it. (And you do, very quickly. Even I had, to some extent.)

Argul drew me aside.

"Yinyay added that she's still able to shrink herself. That's what they missed. She said, once we're all out of here, she'll do it. We can put her back in the carrying pouch."

"Great. That'll be a real help."

"It's all we've got, Claidi."

"I know. I *know*. That's why I said *Great* sarcastically."

And I wished we weren't fighting, too, as we seemed to be. He had that old look from long before, back in the Hulta camp—exasperated at me—but without that other look the exasperation had had, then, what had that been? *Love?*

Has love just run down—stopped—its power drained by this *force field* of Ustareth's?

Then there was a bump. There among the smashed chunks of marble and splintered chairs and confidence, we gaped in alarm.

The bump came again, to show us that we hadn't imagined it. Then Yinyay went into a dire sea-heaving tumble, this way, that way.

"A storm?" asked Ngarbo, looking unenthusiastic.

The light coming in through the cracked windows was still clear.

We crawled over the rolling-about mess, and gazed out.

Sky and ocean were streaming sheer blue. Empty. Not a cloud in sight.

Then, there was a cloud.

It was a carved-looking cloud, deep navy blue, and tall, since it rose in layers like terraces out of the sea in only one place, but also it was moving, getting nearer and larger all the time, and as it did this, the waves sprang away before it, and banged hard against Yinyay, making Yinyay pitch and roll.

The horses, brought down from the stable, started to neigh. I floundered to them and found that Argul and Ngarbo had done the same. We pulled them into a huddle, keeping them as steady as we could, telling them it was all right. Which they didn't believe, and nor did we.

Thu stood guard over us, his eyes burning.

What was it out there?

That's what I thought, just before one whole area of Yinyay yawned wide open in the fastest and most appalling way—

The sea rushed in.

We must all have reacted, but there was no time, because next second we were off our feet, scooped up by the water, swept out into the open sea—!

Helpless. No ring to protect me, or anyone else.

"Claidi, it's all right. Look."

Argul, showing me something. Incredibly wanting me to be interested in the bit of sea we're now lying on before we sink. It *was* quite interesting. It wasn't sea.

We were all on a kind of long metal *tray*, which had just run through into Yinyay and collected us all up, and the sea had come with it so I hadn't seen what it was—

Yinyay had let the invading tray in by opening her side.

I looked back. She had vanished.

"She's shrunk—we've lost her—"

"Looks like it," Argul said.

"Oh, Yinyay," I mourned, gawping down over the tray side into the bottomless blue depths. Would she mind? Would she, bound up with all her magical machineries, as she is when tiny, even *notice?*

Yinyay is a machine. It's people who miss each other, people who panic about drowning.

The navy cloud was still there, and now it didn't look like a cloud. And the tray scoop thing, I saw, had run out from it and was now reeling back to it very fast.

Little wavelets, quite cute, now that the cloud-that-wasn't

seemed to be staying still, frisked over the sides of the tray. We were all drenched. Winter's latest lipstick had run, so she had a purple chin. There's always something to cheer you up, I suppose.

But the Cloud rose up and up, got higher and higher. It *was* formed in terraces, the bottom one huge and resting on the sea, then each next one slightly smaller, rising high above sea level. I tried to count these terraces—three—nine—thirteen? We were being reeled into the lowest one.

A vast shadow, cool in the suddenly felt hot sunlight, pooled over us, the shadow of the towering Cloud.

"It's like—" said Winter.

No one else eagerly demanded to know what it was like.

But Winter said, and now, despite her purple chin, I didn't find her funny. "It's a Tower."

We are in the Tower. We're prisoners. I think so, though They say No, we are *not*—

This room is rather cramped. No window. But of course there's light, the frozen science-magic light I first saw at the Rise, and then at Panther's Halt, and in Chylomba and the Raven Tower.

The worst thing is They have put each of us into a different room, in a different part of Their Tower. They said They did this because of the way the rooms were arranged, and shortage of space, and each room is big enough only for one. Which is true. We can go out—or at least I can, so the others can too(?). This door isn't locked. But this Tower is so massive and confusing and odd, I don't know where to start to look for

Argul in it, or anyone. And that is deliberate, surely, separating us, us not being able to get together, even though They say *No, no.*

It's more than a Tower, of course. It is a ship. An ocean-going ship. The terraces are extraordinary decks, and there are in fact fifteen of them.

At the very top of the dark blue structure rests a peculiar fish—no, animal, which I recognized as we were being reeled in, from books, and just as well I did. It was something I first thought I'd see on my enforced voyage to Ustareth's other landmass with the jungles.

A shark.

It has red eyes up there, too, and a great mouth of pointed white teeth which, I have been told, are scrupulously cleaned once every month.

So it's the Shark Tower?

No, They said, laughing amusedly at my foreign-to-Them ignorance. The ship Tower with the shark symbol is called, like Their Queen, *Old Mother Shark.*

(I am due to meet the Old Mother Shark Queen, it seems, today. [Although They said that yesterday.] We have been here four days since They nabbed us out of Yinyay.)

I do *see* the others. At the evening meal, which is called, here, *Posk.* They speak another language, unsurprisingly, but that makes finding out anything even harder. But also They speak the language of the Towers—mine, or how would I understand Them at all. So They can work out everything we say, and we can't get what *They* say to each other—only I do wonder if Argul may; he seems to know a lot of languages. If he and I

[124]

were together, we could try talking in Hulta, and see if They could fathom that—but we don't get the chance. Because when we meet at *Posk*, They prevent us from talking to each other.

And how do They do that? Simple. We each sit, when in the Posking-room, inside a separate large glass *box*. I mean that each of us, Argul, Venn, Dengwi, Winter, Ngarbo, and I, have a box each. We're not alone in these boxes, though. Each box is about the size of a room—a room much bigger than this one I'm in now. And the Sharkians (what else do I call Them?) join each of us in our box, about twenty or so of Them with every one of us. And there They merrily yatter to us, recommending dishes and pouring us drinks. (This is what They do with me, and what I see Them do with the others. Who mostly look as disturbed by it as I must.)

Beyond every individual glass box you can only hear a faint murmur of the other conversations in the other boxes. And though Argul and I, Dengwi and I, and all of us, can signal to each other—as we did the first time—*They* won't let us out to talk to each other. How They stop us is also simple. Once inside, the glass boxes close. That is, they have an opening like a door through which They escort you, and once everyone is in with their group of Sharkians, the box door seals.

We all wanted to get out at the first Posk. We all jumped about and started hitting the glass—it doesn't give—and shouting. Venn impressively knocked out one of his in-box Sharkians. Winter kicked one of hers and upended some sort of soup on another. But this didn't do any good. And They didn't leave off smiling, our captors, for a moment. Even the knocked-out one.

They just hemmed us in, nodding, laughing, and saying Yes, yes (instead of No, no), until we sat down.

Argul hadn't tried to fight Them, by which I knew he had worked out that it was useless. Dengwi, the same. I didn't because frankly I was too scared—of Them.

There are some Sharkians, too, who obviously have Power jewelry (concealed) which works. Ngarbo was unlucky enough to go for one of these. And so I saw happen to him what my ring had made happen to Jade Leaf—he got flung across his glass box in a showering of lights. Then, ever so sympathetically, They revived him.

So now, at Posk, we all sit and either stay dumb, or else (I at least) try to pry information out of the Sharkians.

They tell you nothing by telling you Everything.

For example, I ask, "Where are we going?" and They say, "The ship runs on the power of the ocean," and go into details of how this water power, or waves or something, gives the ship the energy for movement, and also to anchor her, and how, besides, the energy protects the ship and holds her steady in case of tempests.

They are so powerful. I knew almost at once. They are Ustareth's, her allies, whatever They call their Tower or Their Queen. Apart from anything else, that is why *Their* Power and science work here, right on top of the Force Field. Their power comes from her New Power, stronger than anything she gave us.

She isn't Their ruler, though, as I said. This was another unasked question They answered.

I'd actually asked, Me: "Did Ustareth make this Tower-ship?"

They: "Yes, we are Ustareth's chosen subjects. There are several others like us. Our loyalty is to her, and we are given many benefits, as you see. But we elect our own Queen." (And then on about "Old Mother Shark" etc.)

But, Me: "Others? Like you? Do you mean other Towers?"

They: "There are other Towers."

Me: "Do you mean like the Wolf Tower?"

They (gales of mirth): "*Special* Towers."

Me (being careful how I put it): "You mean REALLY like you?"

They just smiled. But They smile all the time. It's genuinely ghastly.

When I asked if Ustareth had told Them to take us captive, They said "No, no," and continued at vast length how we were NOT captives but guests (so we'd been taken guest, then) and how we were *not* kept apart from each other.

To which I ranted, "Then let me speak to Argul!"

And They shook their heads as if I were a bright three-year-old who'd just said something wrong but cute. (Only in Their case, a bright three-year-old wouldn't be like a me-kind of three-year-old at all.)

So I said, "*Why* won't you let me speak to Argul?"

And They said, "But look, there he is. *Speak.*"

"How *can* I through two layers of glass when you won't even let me leave this box thing??!!!"

"Ha ha ha," They went, "ha ha ha."

Are they just all cuckoo? Very likely.

They're the perfect jailors. But no, it's more sinister than that. It nearly always is.

Despite everything, every *day* I *have* tried to find Argul, or anyone. Wandering over the decks, climbing stairs, and nearly falling in disgusting tanks. Getting lost *under*-deck, getting trapped in elevators (They have them, but these elevators are worse than normal ones; they don't seem to work well, or at least not for me, because the Sharkians use them with no trouble) and screaming and having to be rescued by—Them.

I'll describe Them, the Sharkians.

I've left it till now because well, will you believe me? Yes? Please, please do. I'm not lying. They are—*sharks*.

Twilight's panther in the north could talk. But the thing about that was, it was a clockwork animal.

These—sharks—are actual sharks. Only not quite like the sharks I've read about, of course. Not at *all*. But then these are Ustareth's. (Like the tiger-rabbit-cross vrabburrs, and maybe the original giraffe-horse graffapins, said to be Twilight's invention. All that stuff. Even Grem at the Rise with his leafy hair—and the fur-boy Venn mentioned.)

Sharks are said to be between twelve and forty feet in length, depending on their type and who is telling the tale. They live in water. . . . I expect you know all this. They have awful teeth—three inches long—

The Sharkians have the teeth all right. But They don't have to stay in water. They can walk. Their tail fins at the very bottom are hugely developed and act like (rather clumsy) legs and feet. Also, upright, They aren't twenty or forty feet high. The tallest is about two man-heights—twelve feetish. Some are only eight or nine.

They do like water. There are these slimy, fishy tanks everywhere; you come upon them in the most inconvenient spots—though for the Sharkians presumably they are ideal spots. They can just slip off a stair straight into the lovely, tepid, reeking, murky water—as I have endlessly nearly done.

They each have a room to themselves, and a few spare for shark callers, or for prisoners. The rooms all have a waterbed, by which I mean a big slot of black water to lie in. The "bed" They gave me clings to the side of this water-slot, and I'm terrified of rolling off in the night and into the water. (The bed is only the narrowest mattress. My feet just reach the end. Argul, Venn, Ngarbo and even Winter, who are all taller than me and Dengwi, must overlap uncomfortably.) (Unless they have larger mattresses?)

You get used to the stink. Of the ship, the tanks and slots, Them. Only to Them you don't get used.

How can They talk? And have a whole language, and know my language, too. . . . I see how They can walk, and how They pour out a glass of (fish-flavored) wine or lemonade with one of Their also-overdeveloped side fins. But how, how do They have speech, let alone *laughter*. The upsetting smiles are, of course, built in.

What has she done to Them?

They don't mind. They're not even proud of it; it's just *normal* to—Them.

And though They like to sleep all alone, hence the tiny

rooms, They are sociable with each other, and when you ask a question, the group you're with all reply at once, in completely the same voices and at the same speed, even all drawing breath at the identical moment—like a choir, singing.

What does Argul think of *this?*

Venn maybe can accept it the best. He got used to U's creations at the Rise. And Winter and Ngarbo saw similar (though not quite) things at Chylomba. But Dengwi—

And what do *I* think?

Could they be nice, after all, these ship-sailing, walking, talking sharks? I mean, are They trying to look after us, taking us undoubtedly on toward Ustareth's country, and thinking we really want that—and simply misunderstanding the questions we—I—ask?—and that we like sleeping over water-slots and eating in glass boxes alone with twenty of *Them.*

Ah—it's just come to me—am I right? *They* can speak to each other *inside their minds.* It must be, or how can whole groups all talk at once like that and say exactly the same thing all together in twenty voices. So do They think *we* can do that too, not with them, but amongst *ourselves?* So if we don't find each other on the ship, or talk to each other during *Posk*—we're just being stupid, or mucking about like moody children—

When They first helped us off that tray thing and into the lowest deck, I was petrified by Them. When they spoke, that made it worse. But I remember how Thu was barking and the horses rearing—but the Sharkians started talking to them, too, and Thu and the horses calmed down. Thu even wagged his tail. (Maybe he likes Their smell?) I've seen both horses and our dog since, being groomed and petted by the Sharkians. I'd thought They'd just devour them, and us. They even let me walk Thu, though he certainly seems quite happy to go off again with Them.

Despite how They look, They *talk*, and no matter how I think I feel, am *I*—getting used to Them?

Five of Them just came by, and squashed in the doorway. They said I'm to be taken to meet Their Queen at once. They seemed very thrilled for me, receiving this great honor.

They are not surprised that I want to jot it down here.

"Will any of my friends be there?" I asked, very uneasily.

"No, no," they congratulated me, "just you."

Anyway, I've got no choice.

We went, They and I, along the open deck, which was covered in tanks and pipes and unidentifiable-by-me shark-important things, and into one of the elevators, which are very large and which They can make work.

Up we rushed.

Then, when the door was undone, out I went into absolute—

I hadn't expected it. As I wavered, thinking something dangerous was going on, with all these screeches and drumming sounds, and damp, blue-grey shark forms lumbering everywhere, my sharks said in their chorus, "The Queen is here. She is attending the Fish Races."

She was.

They guided me through bounding sharks waving wild fins

and thumping on the decking—some of Them were taking bets—and up a shark-stair to a raised platform which overlooked a long stretch of water like a canal.

In this, arrowing along, were about thirty large fish, the most gleaming shades of gold and scarlet, or striped like mint humbugs.

Even my escort paused to watch. "See, see, Roserat's in the lead!" They chorused, overcome by evident glee. And then They got so overcome They lapsed into Sharkish—

Some other Sharkians were there then, leading me up to a wide kind of couch. And here, amid the luxurious sopping-wet cushions, and little jets of water, lay the Queen, Old Mother Shark.

You could see she was a Queen. Her top fin, not her head, but almost, was circled by a crown of intricate silver, set with skillfully cut gems—here was one whose Power jewelry wasn't hidden. (I've wondered if the others have Theirs set in back teeth.)

I don't know if she *was* old. Her eyes, small shark eyes, liquid black, unthinkable, may have been old. Her skin was like everyone else's, like a smoky dusk turned to leather.

She was a Queen and I was her prisoner, so I didn't bother to bow. But that felt wrong. She had a real Presence, more than most royalty I've met. Save, of course, for Ironel and Jizania. Is Old Mother Shark just another of these dominant Old Ladies?

"Be seated," she said. And she alone—spoke by herself.

I was shown to a dry cushion.

Like all of Them, she could see me better from the side.

(Shrieks and cries like *Nist-nist* from the lower area—Roserat had won!)

"Tonight," said Old Mother Shark, "we reach the coast."

My already-hurrying heart tried to jump out of my throat and run away. It didn't make it. Never does.

"The coast of *her* country?"

"Yes. Hers." She added, "You will be taken ashore, as she wishes."

"Ustareth wishes," I managed.

"Ustareth," said the Queen.

Another race was starting below. Roserat, a ruby-and-white-dotted fish, was being carried through the crowd by ten prideful Sharkians. She wasn't in water, either, and seemed to be speaking to those she passed, thanking Them probably for Their kind words on her win.

But when the Queen said Ustareth's name, I turned back to her. She said that name like a prayer.

If I'd ever thought I could plead with this lot, I saw now it wouldn't work.

But I said, "What if *I* don't wish to go ashore?"

OMS flicked her crown-fin.

"Where else would you go? Your companions go there."

"Let me see them," I said. "Let me see Argul, and talk to him."

OMS sighed. We were covered in a fog of fishy breath, delightful to everyone—they leaned forward to receive it—but me.

But I probably smell—unusual—to Them, too. They tactfully conceal this.

I said, "You're not going to let us meet, then, until we get ashore."

"That is up to you."

"We can't talk in our heads—we're not telepathic, as you are. *We* can't talk unless we can *hear* each other."

Just then Roserat was borne up to the Queen.

In Sharkian the Queen told Roserat (I think) how well she had done. She stroked Roserat with one fin, and the fish began to sing—or maybe it was her way of purring.

Anyhow, I got up, and when Roserat was taken away, I said, "All right. I suppose I can wait."

Old Mother Shark said, "Her land is called Summer."

"Well, thanks. It's been a great visit." And then I said insolently, "How can you talk?"

"How can *you?* If I tell you how you yourself are able to form words, you will not understand one sentence in a hundred. The same if I try to inform you about us. Ustareth bred us. We are hers. One of several races that are."

"She isn't God, even if she *plays* God."

"No, she is Ustareth," said Old Mother Shark, as if that was enough.

The Sharkians led me away. And by tonight, we shall be there—

Be there.

At least when They put us ashore, I'll be with him.

Why was I afraid to write that? I shall write it again to make sure it's true.

I'LL BE WITH HIM.

THE SHINING SHORE

The navy blue shark ship drew away.

I watched her or it as she or it did so. Her sky-scraping fifteen stories seemed to carve a thin, invisible line along the sky.

It was just after dawn. Everything still mostly palest gold-yellow, like that wine we drank at the House, with Pattoo and Groother. Before we knew how complicated everything was going to get. Again.

But it was a nice dawn.

They had waited until the light came, to put me off ashore.

They sent me, with my companions, in a sort of boat. The Sharkians didn't come. The boat made its own way to the land.

And when we'd got out, it went away again. It had neither oars nor sail.

So, here we are.

I turn and look at my two friends.

"Should I have made more fuss?" I ask them.

How many times have I asked this in the course of my insane "adventures"? How many times have I done it, and got nowhere, or not done it and wondered if I would have got somewhere if I had?

Anyway, neither of these friends of mine has any comment to make.

I kept asking myself, too, if *They* might change their minds, come back. But no, They haven't. And now the ship called *Old Mother Shark* is just a little dark dot on the edge of the wine-yellow, getting-blue sea.

So.

So . . .

I am so angry—and so lost.

Being on this—*place*—is like what I feel inside, really.

Thu wags his tail, and then stops, seeing that I'm not going to throw a stick or encouragingly say, "Yes, go for a run along this charming iron-hard beach."

Mirreen just waits patiently.

And I think of Argul, and I wonderwonderwonder where he *is*.

The night before, I'd been going mad, waiting for us to get to the Continent. I'd also tried to be practical, now that there's no backup from Power jewels or Yinyay. I'd said to Them I wanted journey-food and water. The Sharkians went, "No, no." And now "No, no" really meant *No*, because They wouldn't give me anything at all, and wouldn't tell me where I could get anything.

That night's Posk was different. It was only me and ten Sharkians in one glass box. All the other boxes empty. Hopeless to ask where were all my friends. "They are well," was all I endlessly got. So instead I began to stuff food away in pockets and a bag, for tomorrow. (I knew Argul would have thought of this, too, and perhaps Ngarbo would. But if they weren't getting any Posk-dinner, they might not have had the chance.) *They* watched me do this, and They looked—sorry for me, as if I were a truly pathetic being who'd missed the Whole Point.

No doubt I am and have.

Anyhow, armed with these rations, I then haunted the open deck (the seventh one, I think; I couldn't get any of the elevators to work at all, or would have gone higher). I was trying to see where we were going, to confront the land when it appeared.

In the dark, with the moon not up yet, it was of course invisible.

The weather was calm. I could smell sea, and air. Then I could smell marzipan and oranges—that must have been something left over from Posk. Below, on the lower decks, above me on the upper ones, the Sharkians came and went.

Then the moon did come up, and still I couldn't see any land. And then, I saw it.

Long, curved, glimmering. Impossible to pick out detail. A coast, and then cliffs, it seemed, rising up behind. Very—totally vast.

They anchored about midnight, and some miles out.

Then I said were we going to be put off there, now, and again got a logical answer: No, at dawn.

I considered if this was being very fair, or some other plot.

(See how I think now. It isn't surprising, is it.)

I said again, "Let me see Argul."

"Yes, yes," They said. Which still meant, "No, no."

I went to sleep in the end, so tired I could hardly stand up, curled on a softish bundle of some sharky stuff or other on the deck. Wish I'd done that before—it was much better than the water-slot mattress. (I had also tried again to find the others, and failed, as you see. Then in my dreams I did find them, but none of them would talk to me; they walked away. Argul did this in the dream, too.)

I woke up again at first light.

Going to the rail, I craned out, and saw the land. It was like a long, curved rim of a steel plate, mistily glowing.

Was it distance that made it look so regular?

Sharkians came and offered me breakfast (which is called Grob, though I don't know why I bother to note this now). I shook my head, just drank some water. Which was stupid—it had been another opportunity to grab some Grob for the journey. From the looks of it, I was going to need it, we all were, ashore.

Then I stood about, waiting for the others to come out, getting a bit excited. I thought, *they're late*. I thought, *We'll be able to speak to each other even before we get put in the boats or whatever.*

No one appeared, however. Only Sharkians going up and down on Their fat fins.

And then some came up again and the boat was ready, so I went with Them to this outside elevator thing, which had a boat in it. But no one was in the boat.

"Where are my friends? Where is my husband?"

"Everything is all right," said the eight Sharkians standing beside me.

"No, it *isn't* all right. *Where is Argul?*"

"Argul is well. There is no need for you to worry."

I turned and gripped one of Them. Have you ever had to try to grip a dampish, thirteen-foot-high shark? It's not easy. My hands slid and slipped and I couldn't really *get* any of it to stay in my grasp, but I managed to maul it a bit and it made distressed noises. I thought too late, thank heavens it wasn't one of the ones with Power jewels.

"TELL ME!!"

They told me, even the one I was grappling with, that I had nothing to be worried about.

It was then that four other sharks brought Thu and Mirreen along the deck, and I broke off and the one I'd grabbed got away from me.

(Apart from the jewels, They're peaceful. They don't ever hit back. Or have They forgotten how? One chomp of those teeth, and I really wouldn't have had any worries.)

I ran across to Thu, who leapt at me. We had a touching re-union. I stroked and patted Mirreen. They were both in excel-lent condition, as I'd already seen on other days.

The Sharkians now wanted all of us to get in the boat, and I resisted, and so Thu resisted, and Mirreen reared.

"I won't go anywhere," I shrieked, "without the others!"

Then I got an actual reply.

"They have already crossed to shore."

"Wh-aa-tt?"

"Last night," said the now-twelve Sharkians. "All have gone to land but you."

"Why *not* me?"

"You slept."

"Then why didn't you *wake* me—"

"You are awake now."

I didn't believe this was the reason. Or are They really so crazy that it is?

I made sure I hadn't misunderstood. Hadn't. After all, the land was where we were all supposed to go, as per Her instruc-tions.

At last, I got in the boat with Thu and Mirreen.

Then it was lowered by the elevator out over and down the sides of all the decks, into the water, and the sun was about to come up.

I just kept hoping the others would have stayed together—and stayed to wait for *me*. (Unlike in my dreams.)

The sun was rising as we moved forward, over on the left. The water spangled and parted before the boat.

The shore came close and closer.

What is it made of? It soon looked entirely like a soft-shining greyish metal. I expected this to change as we got nearer, but it didn't and hasn't.

When the sea grew shallow, I could see a sloping shelf of the metalness below, under the water. I couldn't see fish there, or seaweed, or anything like that.

The boat ground onto the shore.

Which was empty.

"This is the wrong place," I said, trying to sound reasonable. "You must find the right one."

The boat didn't talk back, although all things were possible, by now. Nor could I make it change direction. I tried everything I could think of.

Then Thu jumped out onto the metal plate of shore. Mirreen was getting restless again—and I felt it, too, as if the mechanical boat were trying to force us off—and then it did. It started this shuddering, almost bucking like a horse itself. So then I had to get Mirreen quickly up the thoughtfully provided ramp, and out, before she got hurt. I then meant to turn and "reason" with the boat again. But the moment I was out, it was off. It had been useless anyway. It must have had its "orders." It had doubtless brought me exactly where it was supposed to. Because the Sharkians were always awkward, but They were *never* inefficient.

I was meant to be here alone.

The boat disappeared quickly away and back into the ship's side, swallowed by the lowest deck.

I looked up the metal beach at the rising metal cliffs shining mildly in the morning.

Should I walk along the shore, see if I can find anyone? But the slightly curving land went round to the horizon on both sides, miles of it, it seemed. And since it was completely featureless, anything on it would have been obvious at once, and nothing was there.

I began to see it all. The Sharkians had separated us from the start. Now each of us has been brought, secretly from the others, I think, and each to a different place on the coast. We are all far enough from each other, we won't find a trace.

That must be it—that *is* it. I know.

And so here I sit, and now the dot of the Shark ship has become itself a speck and vanished.

Strangely, the sun on this metal plate isn't getting agonizingly hot. It's only pleasantly warm. And the little wavelets cream on the shore as they would on any decent beach.

Thu and Mirreen have been fed; those sharks did tell me that. And I'm not hungry. So the best thing is going to be—the only thing worth doing under these circumstances. We must find a way to climb the cliffs and see what lies beyond.

THROUGH THE WALL

To me, it looked as if there was no way up at all. The metal surface ran in for perhaps about a quarter mile, and then the metal cliffs rose sheer from it.

Really, they weren't cliffs. More—walls?

I led Mirreen, and Thu padded along at my side. I was very glad they were with me. And I kept talking to them, off and on.

"What we need is a path, a way up."

By then we'd got to the foot of the cliffs. I stood staring up and up. No, *not* cliffs. They *were* probably walls. Very, very high. And totally smooth.

I thought, does anyone else ever come here? Proper shipping, blown off course in storms, trying to make landfall here, getting discouraged by the metal and going away?

Thu barked.

"Hello, Thu."

He shook his ruff at me, and went bounding off to the left.

"Thu—*no*. Come back—"

I realized it would be pretty hard to lose him on the empty shore, but even so—

He's not as obedient as Hulta dogs are. I suppose he isn't a Hulta dog. He kept going.

Hurrying after him, Mirreen and I found he had come to a different area of cliff/wall. It looked rougher and had two long, almost pillars, side by side, rising up about twenty feet.

And then the pillars moved. They drew slowly apart. And there between them was a high, slim door.

"It's a door," I told Thu and Mirreen.

Thu looked impressed. He flag-waved his tail.

So I walked right up to the door. It was closed, of course, and made of a sort of translucent greenish *something*. It felt silky to the touch. And though almost see-through, I *couldn't*, squinting, see anything through it. Nor was there anything *on* it, like a handy doorknob or even door-knocker. The whole personality of this door was, See, here I am, showing myself to you—and you can't get me to open, can you?

I glanced at my ring. The diamond that means so much because Argul gave it to me, and because it has twice saved my life! But that sometimes, like now, I hate, too, because *she* made it.

A Power ring with no power, or none of the New Power Ustareth now uses.

"Well, this is thrilling."

Thu had sat down. He was looking at me, wondering why I didn't open the door so we could go through.

"Sorry, I don't think I can get it open—"

The green door opened.

Just like THAT.

Was it so straightforward? It just needed to hear that one word "open"—and it would?

Thu and I stared through the opened door.

What was there, starting only a few feet beyond the door, was another wall of metal, only this one wasn't the same. It humped and curved over. And, despite still going up as high as the outer wall-cliffs (which was about three hundred feet, I'd say) this had a *path* running up over it. The path was white stone, or looked like it. In fact, all this was like something natural, a hill with a sloping roadway.

It should be possible to ride up the Road to the top of the Hill.

I tried the road-surface first, to make sure it would be all right for Mirreen. It was. So I mounted up, and rode easily up the slope, with Thu trotting behind.

What did I anticipate at the summit? I wasn't sure. What I *found*, when we got there, was this: a plateau.

This was flat as a tabletop, though, and white like the "stone" path. It was laid with paving, each marble-looking slab faultlessly regular and about six feet on each side. And that— was it. This paved table stretched away and away to left and right along the Hilltop, and away and away and *away* in front, until it melted into the sky.

I turned and looked back then, the way we'd come.

No shock to see the green door, far down at the base of the wall, had now 1) closed, and 2) disappeared from view.

Otherwise there was the crest of the outer cliff/wall, some distance off now because of the Hill's slope, and over *that* all I could see was the blue ocean, miles of it, and as empty as the cloudless blue sky.

Had everyone else done a climb like this, up to this plateau-table? Or were there different obstacles in the spots they'd been taken to?

I feel very removed from them. (Yes, from Argul, too.) Is that odd? It's only that now, I really am on my own.

But there was still nowhere to go but forward, so that's what I did. The paving was so good, I even set Mirreen to a fast trot to match Thu's.

(He ran with his nose down, trying to pick up some scent or other. But to me, all I could smell was the faint tang of the sea, and as we went on, that faded.)

I kept the sun on my left, so my forward direction was still south. I could have gone off east or west, but that seemed only likely to keep me going round the outside of the wall. Unless, of course, it didn't circle all or most of the whole landmass—but Ustareth's manner of doing things always seems Huge in some way.

The left-hand sun got higher. Soon it began to be hot. The air burned with its own light, and the marble or whatever glared, though not as badly as real white marble in direct sunlight.

There was absolutely nothing on the paved plateau but for our three figures, and the increasingly short shadows we threw.

I started to think about the desert I'd first escaped into. The dusty, blistered treks Nemian and I had to make.

And the plateau didn't change. And it showed no sign of coming to an end.

It was almost noon, the sun getting to its worst, when a tree appeared at the horizon! (Look, Thu! A tree!)

Unsensibly, perhaps, I sent Mirreen flying at a canter at this tree, and Thu, yards of tongue hanging out (a wonder he didn't trip over it) cantered with us. And we reached the tree and—

"What is *that?*"

It wasn't a tree. But also, it was.

Like the paving, the Tree was of white marble-stuff. In shape it *was* like a tree, resembling a tall and spreading cedar, but it had no leaf-needles. Purely put there for decoration then, how quaint.

Then the Tree did this very clever and helpful thing. (The first of three.)

First, out from all the overhead spread boughs, opened these wonderful kind of sunshades. They were all tones of turquoise or hyacinth blue or palest plum, and the moment they got between us and the sun, there fell coolness and relief.

The next thing was a fountain-spray out of the Tree's "trunk." It looked like clear water and Thu thought so too—

"No—wait—" I tumbled off Mirreen and tried to get hold of him. No, he really is not obedient. (Another one who won't be a slave.) He was already lapping up the water where it formed a pool on the ground. He seemed to find it refreshing, and when I hauled him off, just went dancing round the Tree and started again on the other side. It did *seem* to be water, tasted like it and so on. So—I too drank some. (Like the worst kind of idiot in a story, but I was gasping for a drink, and had been trying to save the pitiful amount I'd stored from the last Posk and Grob.) In fact, the water tasted very clean, and sweet. In the end I let Mirreen, too, have what she wanted from the pool.

When we stopped, the fountain did. But then something else happened.

I gazed in disbelief as ripe yellow fruits, rather like peaches, began to bud out on the Tree's lower boughs, grow large, and then hang there, filling the air with a delicious peachy-orangy scent.

They might be the trap, might be poisonous.

I'd risked the water, but this I truly didn't trust. (Didn't trust any of it.)

So I wouldn't pick the tempting fruits, and when Thu began long, running bounces at the lowest ones, trying to reach and knock them off, I called him so sternly to heel he obeyed.

Dejectedly, he and I shared a small piece of stale pie.

Mirreen I'd been able to bring nothing for. I'd just have to hope there was some grass soon. I mean real grass, not something made of metal or stone or some other ungrasslike material.

We did rest for a while in the welcome shade. I sat on the paving, and the cooling sunshades fluttered a little, like soft wings fanning us. A while later I saw the ripe fruit we hadn't taken was shrinking away again into the marble boughs. After a few minutes it was quite gone, just the hunger-making scent left behind.

Before we left, I did think to fill up the water flask I'd stolen from Old Mother Shark. The moment I got near the Tree trunk, the fountain helpfully spouted out again. Then we went on, over the paved tabletop.

Afternoon was hot and heavy. The sky grew pale at its center, and there was a heat haze smoking at each of the four ends of the neverending plateau. By now the wall was long out of sight. Any way you looked was only paving, and sky.

When the sun went down in a few hours, I decided, we would "make camp" as best we could, here in the middle of—literally—nowhere. I didn't want to travel in the dark, afraid I might lose our direction if the moon was late.

Nothing else happened, except we passed another Tree (more an oak than a cedar) and had a brief rest there and drink of water. It, too, put out (honey and purple tone) sunshades, had a fountain, and grew us some irresistible (red) fruit I wouldn't let any of us go near. We didn't stay long.

The sunset, when it came, was vivid, like the colors of all the sunshades and fruits. And when it was over, the night dropped cool as rain, then cold as sleet, as I'd guessed it might.

So we stopped, and here we are by the small leer of a fire

I've managed to make on the paving. No magic ring to give light, but I've written by firelight before.

To every side of us stretches this threatening emptiness, ghostly in starlight, and overhead a black, so far moonless sheet of sky.

The stars look strange. Not the stars I remember, but so they did too above the jungles of the Rise.

How is Venn coping with this? What is Dengwi doing—does she—or Winter, come to that—even know how to light a fire? Perhaps they've come across marble Trees too, and eaten the fruit, and are lying dead—no. I will NOT think of that. Anyway, I don't believe that is why *She* brought us here, I mean, just to bump us off. In a disgusting way, we're being cared for. So probably I *could* have stuffed myself with fruit and—

Oh!!!!!

I leapt up, staring, as a great bird wheeled over. It came from nothing—or from the dark horizon. Its wings gave a weird, dull flash as they caught the eerie starshine. Then it turned and soared away again—inward, southward, the way I am trying to go.

So something *is* there, proper bird-and-animal-supporting landscape, perhaps sanity and some answers. It's just a matter of keeping on.

But for how long?

I dreamed that night about Argul. He was riding fast on his horse that has the same color scheme as he does, the horse he bought at Peshamba and still hasn't named. In the dream, everything was dark, and I couldn't see what he was riding across or through, but I called to him and never thought he'd hear. Yet he reined in at once, and looked around him. But he didn't see me, and really, I wasn't there—

This dream made me feel bad. I shook it off with difficulty as we set out again over the paving, the sun once more to the left.

Before midday we'd passed six Trees; I counted them. A "beech," a "willow" (sunshades trailing to the ground), three "palm trees," and another "oak." We had some water at the beech and the oak. At the oak, I thought, Why not? And I ate a fruit. It was apple-green and tasted of apple and green plums, also grapes, I think. Thu watched me, trying to understand my sudden evil selfishness in not sharing the fruit with him. At midday, about two hours later, feeling fine and no hint of having been poisoned, I let him have the one I picked for him, and gave Mirreen another. There are still no ill effects, so unless it's unbelievably slow-acting poison, it isn't poison at all. The fruit is also more strengthening than just fruit usually is. We have a lot of energy.

Anyway, during the afternoon, a big flock of birds came dazzling over, high up, black on blue.

And after we'd seen these, we began to see lots of birds all the time. They whirled over our heads, going seaward where we'd come from, then coiled back and returned away into the south.

There was the scent, by then. It was glorious. Imagine every sort of perfumed flower you can think of, all the favorites, and every tastiest fruit, and mixed together, but nothing not going with anything else. Then add the freshest fragrance of earliest morning, with dew down, young green leaves on every tree—and more. Things I couldn't be sure of—but one like an actual perfume, but so subtle it was just right—oh, and that exciting, glittery smell of rain at the end of a hot day—

All that.

It came in soft waves along the paving. It made you—happy. Thu was ecstatic, jumping and playing. Mirreen tossed her head and wanted to go more quickly. I held her back in case—because I knew that soon the tabletop must finally reach its end, and despite the scents, we didn't know in what.

The sun was well over and low, on the right. The sky was growing roselike there, and enormous tides of birds now, uncountable numbers of them, swarmed above.

And then I saw that what was coming up from the horizon now was, of all things, this ornamental marble railing, like the balustrade of some terraced garden.

Beyond, smoldering, arriving sunset stretched, and I couldn't be sure, but it seemed all open sky—

I still, though, let Mirreen go faster. Very quickly we were there.

The balustrade came up breast-high on her. I sat on her back, and looked across.

And I wanted to cry.

Because, even in the ending of full daylight, I could see enough. And Ustareth made this. Ustareth.

AS SUN IS TO THE CANDLEFLAME

The Hulta have a saying, that something that is a million times better than all other versions of it—for example an especially brilliant horse—is "as sun is to the candleflame." In other words, ordinary horses are useful, glowing candleflames, but this one horse is like the blazing sun.

When I looked over the railing, into the country Ustareth created, I knew that everywhere else—everywhere—is only a candleflame.

Is this why she called it Summer?

From up there, I could see a long way. The plateau tabletop is very high. (And the way down was really unnerving, a sort of ramp, which seemed to go on for many tilting, almost-vertical miles. But right then I didn't even notice.)

I've said the sun was getting ready to leave. It was forming a lake of crimson over there, and the sky above faded up through degrees of crimson to a final delicate blossom-pink.

Everything below was softening into shadow. But before the evening claimed it, in the last light I saw this sweep of shadowed green grasslands, zebra-striped across and across by its bands of wild flowers, powderings all the colors of the sky. And this was like Peshamba, those meadows as you get near, but here on such a colossal scale, vast, going on and on, and curving off into the distance on either side.

It was all in a just-visible curve, the landscape, winding in slightly, like a plate rim, as the shoreline had—but I was seeing it from so far up. Down there the curve wouldn't be noticeable.

Still enough light, the rest of the sky so clear—I could make out woodlands massed like clouds lying on the land. And they were green and coppery even as they darkened—and some were damson color, and some were royal blue, so I blinked, but they were still royal blue, like flowers.

I could see waters and rivers glimmering through. I could see a lake like a diamond that the sky made into a ruby.

As the land rolled on toward the south, far away I noted another boundary. It was a forest, I thought, gigantic, running off and along, going to blackness now, so the curving circle it formed was made more obvious. And, then, beyond the circling forest, which lay inside the circling meadows, was something else I couldn't make out. But all these circles that from up here looked mathematically perfect. (As the table-terrace is, I think. And the wall, and even the coast.) Summer must be, then, exactly round. Like—an enormous coin resting on the ocean.

At the inmost center—hundreds of miles off, it looked—and if it *is* the center—could I just make out the shape of a circle of mountains? I'm not sure. If they are, they seem very high, higher than any mountain I've ever heard of.

Then all the west became so red it was as if a new color had been invented, too.

The landscape soaked up crimson from the sky.

I dismounted from a crimson Mirreen, and sat by the railing, and a crimson Thu sat beside me. We watched the glory of the sun, which is like her land of Summer, swell and go out in long, echoing chords.

And then the sky lifted even higher, and was crystal green, on which the stars appeared as the birds left it.

And then came the heavenly scents of night, flowing up from the valley below.

We had some fruits I'd brought from the last oak. I didn't try the ramp in the dark. I didn't light a fire. It was warm, just right, with a cool breeze smelling of jasmine.

Oh, I hate her more for this.

How could she? Make something so beautiful and—*good*—and meanwhile hurt the ones who loved her, so heartlessly. Did all the sensitivity and truth in her go into *this*, so nothing and no one else could matter?

Daylight, and it's all even more beautiful, and I refuse to describe it any more. (But there *were* blue trees, and lavender ones and—)

"We have to get down that ramp thing," I remarked, off-hand, to Thu.

He looked unimpressed. The ramp seemed downright dangerous. *This* is where she'll kill me?

I remembered in the north, the way I was shown down through the *inside* of a cliff. Was there anything like that here?

We tried for a time to find something. Couldn't.

Where the ramp started, the balustrade had an inviting gap in it, but just looking down the ramp made me feel sick.

If the ring had worked, I could have got down with no trouble. I had a feeling I could have got Thu and Mirreen down with me, too. When we'd had hold of Dengwi, the ring and the sapphire had just lifted her, too. Live things were obviously different from the books I'd tried with first.

Anyway, no point in thinking of the ring, it didn't work anymore.

And then—

Every time I reckon things can't possibly become stranger or more alarming—they do.

They did.

"Look at those birds, Thu, flying up, lucky things. They seem to appear out of nowhere, don't they. Oh, they're coming right toward us. *Duck, Thu!*"

We ducked, and behind us, with a clatter, the three birds that, even then I'd half seen were *not* birds, landed on the terrace just behind us.

Thu and I turned. Mirreen turned, and shied.

There they stood. In their robes of stone, their metal

masks, one in a hat like a melon and one in a hat like an umbrella wrong way up, and one in a hat like a black enamel halo.

Before I could decide to throw myself straight off the high terrace, they had us. In their (unbelievably) strong, long, wide stone sleeves.

Up we went, Thu howling and kicking, Mirren neighing and kicking, me silent and unmoving from terror. Up and over and out, into blue morning space.

SUMMER

Down we blew.

Just air rushing.

Then the rush of the earth. (If it even is, here.)

One cloud I somehow saw unrolling—and then the tumbling green and amethyst and *sky blue* trees and the every-color flowers—and all of it flying up to meet us as we fell.

The landing was soft.

Hadn't thought it would be. But it was.

And instantly the stone sleeve-arms let go, and I fell straight over, facedown in some poppies, and lay there.

Then I jumped up.

I confronted—it—*them*. They'd alighted in a neat row. Mirreen, freed, was shaking her head, and then she did rear, and went racing off through the poppies and wild red lupins. But my legs were shaking too much to run after her. Thu slunk over to me, his belly to the ground. The grass came to the tops of his legs; he seemed to think he wanted to hide in it, but had the goodness of heart to come to me first.

I stroked the tense fur between his ears. I told him he was wonderful. Then I went right up to the stone statues from Peshamba, and confronted them.

Now they seemed to be only statues again. Three unmoving figures placed for some unknown reason in a meadow.

When I pushed one, I hurt my hand on its ungiving hardness, that was all. When I tried to pull at their mask-faces, they stayed put.

Then I tried walking away briskly through the flowers. Thu hurried after me. But the statues didn't.

Then we ran. It helped us, as it had Mirreen—though I couldn't see where she'd got to.

When I stopped and looked back, they were still there, the statues, stopped, now quite a long way off. The sun glinted smooth on their masks.

They're Hers.

All this time they have, somehow, followed me. They're what? Guards? They'll let me do as I want providing that fits with what I'm *meant* to do. I had to reach these ringed valleys and hadn't got down—so they brought me.

We found Mirreen behind a group of great golden-green trees (I don't know what type, perhaps a new invented one), and by then the statues had gone from view over a shoulder of the meadow. Mirreen was eating grass. It looked nourishing. I was fairly sure there would soon be more fruit for Thu and me.

The crazy thing is—it's very difficult to be depressed, here. I mean I'm anxious, and I wish Argul were with me. Or anyone. (Maybe not Winter. Or Venn, really . . .) But.

It's so beautiful, and this air, and the sunlight and the scents. One can't avoid looking at things and—liking them a lot.

And we're not harmed, are we? And the direction is now crushingly obvious. Forward, to the center of this massive little coin-shaped continent. While if we "go wrong" I'm sure some helpful statue will suddenly appear and haul us back on the right path.

Everyone else, for all their different reasons, will be going that way. Except, maybe, Dengwi? Because what has any of this to do with her?

Thu and I saw some dapply deer not long ago. Thu cheered up, though I persuaded him (clutching his collar) not to give chase. But the deer took no notice of us, anyway. And later I saw a fox curled up like a ginger cat in the sun, asleep.

We came to the Breakfast Wood—what else do I call it?— about an hour after we landed in the ring-valleys of Summer.

It seemed to be just one more stretch of perfect woodland, wending along the banks of a broad, sparkly stream.

There were ferns and bellflowers, and then we smelled another fragrance. Thu forgot all caution and dashed headfirst into the wood.

I was less keen. I thought the smell indicated someone, or

several someones, were in it already, cooking a large meal. And that could mean anything. On the other hand, it might mean someone who'd give us food—?

The woodland was dense only with flowers, the trunks of the trees wide-spaced. Sunlight hung in golden chains.

At first there were just the green leaves growing lushly from the boughs, and here and there a climbing rose or vine. Then I came to a tree, and saw that the lowest branch, which was level with my shoulder, had put out leaves of—well, like green *glass*. And on these glass leaves were lying hot, smoking sausages, and thick slices of ham. It's no use my apologizing for telling you this. There they were.

Some of the sausages and ham had, actually, dropped down on the ground, still on their glass leaves, which hadn't broken. Thu was busily eating.

"Thu, I don't know if—"

But now that tree over there, with coppery leaves, was putting out extra coppery leaves that were hardening even as I watched—to copper. And out of each leaf was appearing a small rounded thing, which then grew much larger, and golden, and filled the air with the nonresistible smell of exactly what they seemed to be, which was fresh-baked buttered bread. And there now, there were eggs coming out there, hot boiled eggs in brown shells. And there another sort of gold, an opened honeycomb spilling honey.

More than hunger now, fascination. I wandered forward, and soon reached a tree that had begun to form, not leaf-glass plates, but furled leaf-glass goblets, and in them stood pale amber tea or thick dark chocolate, and there was one, all ready to pour cream—

I just started laughing.

Thu glanced up, gave me a withering look, and buried his fangs in another kindly just-fallen-Thuward chunk of ham.

It was like the marble Trees up on the plateau. Only better. And so playful, generous. If this was hers, then it, like all the rest, was not at all like her. And yet—who else could have the scientific ability to create such absurd and annoyingly marvelous things? (Twilight was fairly clever, or seemed so. Think what she created. Richly jeweled hills, an unfriendly place in the sky, and more Rules.)

In the end, I *didn't* resist. I don't often eat meat now (got out of the way of it at the Rise, where even the cheese and butter were made from nuts or plants). The same is true here—must be—the trees themselves are producing everything, so the meat, too—which looked and smelled and (Thu thought) tasted of meat—couldn't *be* meat, could it? Anyway, I had hot bread and honey—and even picked a goblet of chocolate, which the royalty had been fond of at the House. It was all terrific. It was all totally real. Only it can't have been, not in that way.

For one thing Thu ate so much—he was on to fish pancakes before I got him to stop—I thought he'd be sick. But he wasn't. He was just bursting with energy.

Later, when we'd gone on along the stream, which flows toward the south, there was something rather the same yet even odder.

About fifty feet off across the meadows, I could see more deer feeding from leafy trees. Then suddenly a creature came bounding over a hill like a banana-yellow arrow. I got hold of Thu. It was, I thought, some sort of big cat, perhaps a leopard.

I expected it, of course, to run into and bring down an unfortunate deer, and the rest of them to scatter and fly.

(From Argul and the Hulta, I know enough to understand it would undoubtedly be more interested in that than in me, M, and T. But even so I was glad the now quite-wide stream was between us.)

Then I saw the deer weren't running away at all. No, they just carried on feeding. The leopard, or whatever it was, stalked majestically through them, ignoring them, until it reached what looked like a larch tree.

I was fifty, sixty feet away, as I say, and didn't risk going closer. But the side of the larch—seemed to open, and something gradually eased out. It looked like a huge piece of meat. Not the kind I'd been offered in the morning, either. This was definitely stronger stuff, and raw—the correct sort of lunch for a leopard.

Maybe I mis-saw.

But really I don't think so.

Later on, I saw something stranger. Well, ENTIRELY strange.

What I saw, and again I seriously doubt you'll believe me, but please do, I did, was a tree, walking.

In fact, five trees, walking.

What a sight! I mean, they simply came over a slope in front of me, and for a moment I didn't know what they were or what I was looking at. And then I did.

They moved by means of their roots, which of course were out of the ground. They used them in a sort of coiling, snakelike wriggle, and glided jerkily past me. Perhaps they turned their leafy heads to look at me—for all I know, they did. Do they have invisible eyes? To see where they're going? Can they—or any of the animals I've seen—speak, as the sharks could?

I don't know how much ground we've covered. The meadows don't change to anything else, though they change their flower colors, long drifts of aquamarine, of blush pink, whole hours of burning coral and marigold—woods come and go, some *really* going (I've seen it three or four times now), getting up and walking off—can they *all* do this? Slender clouds sometimes banner over on the gentle breeze.

It's afternoon.

It's—Heaven.

Yes, it is heaven. Even in the House, where they never spoke of God, or gods who may be expressions of God, there was still this idea of heaven, an exquisite place where everything would be lovely for everyone. For the slaves and servants, I think it was meant to be the sort of final reward we'd get after we were all dead of overwork. That is—we had to earn it, and might not.

This heaven is here on the earth, or at least floating in the sea.

I wonder where the others are? How do they feel? What do they *think* of this?

And what do we think of—Her?

Late, and a sunset even better than yesterday's—and then the cool, green dusk. Still keeping to the south-going stream, which is almost a small river now. When along the bank came walking what I have named the Dinner Forest.

Thu greeted it with a happy puppyish yap. I was riding Mirreen quite slowly, and the forest, of exactly forty trees, moved slowly to meet us. Thu was in there first, and then the forest halted. I watched the great taloned roots digging down into the ground. Perhaps the trees would get a cooling drink at the stream while we had dinner?

You could already smell the dinner.

Need I say, it was spectacular.

There were ten choices of soup, ten of main dishes and vegetables, ten of desserts and sweets, and ten of drinks.

"Thu—stop it! Stop *eating!!!*"

Ustareth is my mother-in-law (what a thought) and we are her guests (taken guest again) and will this all poison us in the end? Or is she only thinking we'll conveniently burst?

Fireflies, scores of them, gave us candles as we dined. Enough, too, to give me light as I scribble.

One nightingale, then others, sang across the meadows.

The moon rose, slim and like a bow.

Oh, Argul.

And oh, Ustareth.

✦ ✦ ✦

The statues are back. All of them. There are thirteen. I've counted them. No proper approach either, they were *just there.*

What happened was, the Dinner Forest stayed. It folded up what hadn't been used and became solely treelike. The moss was thick and soft by the stream, and I thought it had become more so. Warm, soft weather, fine for sleeping out. (I keep remembering what was said at Peshamba—about someone stealing all the good weather for private use—) Thu and I got ready to sleep, and I hoped he would stay close—and Mirreen. Even if I felt I should, tethering either of them to anything didn't seem a wise idea. Because tie them to a tree, and then what if the tree decides to walk off—?

Anyhow, it was peaceful, and the nightingales sang me to sleep.

The moon was far down in the west when Thu woke me, barging up.

Through the standing trees I could see some pale forms loping along. I thought they were wolves. I perhaps sillily thought, They don't need to come after us; the trees keep them fed. Wolves, anyway, are all right, unless starving. These looked sleek and healthily wild. They simply wolfed along on their own moon-called business.

And Thu was very eager to go with them.

"Sorry, Thu, but no. I know they're your half brothers. But."

Half brothers. Like Venn and Argul. Half brothers of the Wolf Tower—

I felt a painful roll of loneliness go through me for Argul. No matter if this were heaven, how I missed him. I hadn't even dreamed of him again.

And then there came this disturbance in the air inside the forest, which took my mind off everything else. What was it? Was it little miniature moths, columns of them, dancing there in the dregs of sinking moon? That's what it looked like. But six columns. Then eight—nine—

Thu growled. Mirreen raised her head from the sweet grass and trampled.

I got up and went to her, and in that second, ten, eleven, twelve, thirteen moth columns all fizzed with moonish light—and there stood Ustareth's guard-watchers, the masked statues from Peshamba.

I yelled. To my disheartenment rather, Thu—*wagged his tail.*

"All right," I said, "what now?"

And then I saw—that each of the mask-faces had now opened a pair of wide blue firefly eyes.

Watchers indeed. I moved, the eyes followed me.

So did I run? No. Again I walked up to them. I counted them carefully. As I stood in front of each, the eyes looked down at me, then looked sideways at me as I moved on.

"What do you want?"

Luminous and unnerving, the blue eyes all met mine now as I turned from one to the other.

Was I afraid? Oddly, no, not anymore. I felt finally more *curious.*

And so in the end I walked right up to one, the one in the melon hat. It was much taller than me, but now it bowed over, so I could stare right in at its eyes.

I'm not sure what I expected. I think, to see another pair of eyes (Hers?) looking back at me from behind the mask-eyes. And surely that would have scared me? I don't know. And it isn't what I saw.

Inside the first pair of eyes—

I really stared. Then I leaned forward, surprising myself, I suppose, and put my face up close to the mask. I looked right in through the eyes of the statue.

And there beyond I saw Venn, sitting by a campfire, and across from him sat Dengwi.

"Venn!" I exclaimed.

And Venn jumped. He raised his head and looked around. Then I heard him speak. Heard him clearly, as if he were only an arm's length away.

"Am I losing my mind?" he said.

And then Dengwi, "No, I heard it, too."

"It sounded like Claidi."

"Yes," she said. "But this is a strange place. Full of high-science magic, and tricks."

"And I was thinking of her," he said. He leaned on a tree, moodily. (They were in a wood like the Dinner Forest, and through the trees I could see other meadows, all white flowers burning in thin moonlight.)

Dengwi just put another stick onto the fire.

I thought, They're not fighting anymore. I thought, Should they have lit that fire? And how did they get the wood—does it *hurt* these trees to do that?

But I didn't speak aloud now. To them I was unseen, my voice one more game Heaven was playing with them.

"Yes," said Venn. "I behaved badly to her. I behaved like a fool and a—what is it, that word she used to use? An okko, something like that. Hulta word. *Hulta*. I was jealous," he said. "I was a bloody disgrace."

"You want Claidi," said Dengwi, cool and still there in the dark.

"Oh, yes. I told her on Yinyay. But then wasn't the time. I mean the time had gone. No, it hadn't ever existed. The first time, at the Rise, it was worth a try. But I wish I'd kept quiet, this second time."

"And I wish I'd spoken to her," Dengwi murmured.

"What do you mean?"

"No," said Dengwi. "My secret. I shan't tell you."

To my amazement Venn didn't try to belittle Dengwi for her silence.

"That's honest," he said. "I respect that."

I could just imagine if *I'd* said it—or if *she* had, a short while ago.

But then, she has this presence, Dengwi. She sat there truly like a royal creature of the night. She'd accused *him* of his royalness, but she looks more royal than he does!

They've *certainly* stopped fighting.

I sensed between them the seed of companionship. The same way he'd fallen for me, when I was the only new woman he'd seen in years, now he's come round to her, because they are alone here together, and that unites them in many ways. (I wonder when they did decide to call a truce? How friendly are they now?) He doesn't seem as upset as I'd have anticipated. Has Dengwi calmed him down?

Also, puzzled, I wanted to say, How is it you two are together, but Argul and I—

But I didn't speak. Of course not.

How could I again, out of thin air? Even if I swore to them it was really me, they couldn't see me and they'd never think it was.

"Well," said Venn, "let's get some rest."

"You sleep," she said. "I'll watch."

"No, then *I'll* keep watch—" all gallantly bad-tempered.

She laughed. Have I heard her laugh before? Must have. It's a good laugh, and I don't remember it. But Venn—*smiled*.

"Fine. You watch first then."

He lets her have her own way, lets her tell *him* what they should do.

This ruffled me. (Even like that, peering sorcerously at them through the eyes of a statue!)

I stepped back, and thought, *That's enough*. And—the eyes of the statue *shut*. It was just the blank mask now, as it had always been before. Then it straightened back up to its full nine feet tall.

So I looked at the others, and saw that only two still kept their eyes open.

I walked, slowly, to the one in the umbrella hat, and as I got near, it too bowed over, and there were the eyes all ready to be gazed in at.

I stared in—and there they were, as I'd half already known. So someone's kept up the fights.

"You're never satisfied, girl," said Ngarbo, standing and frowning.

"*Satisfied?* With *what?* And don't call me *girl!*"

"Woman then," he said.

"Don't call me *woman,*" she shouted. "I am your superior, a Raven Tower Princess."

"Sure," said Ngarbo. "And I'm a kangaroo."

(What's a kangaroo?)

"You might just as well be. You are no help, Ngarbo."

"No. Like when I found the island in the storm that time. Like when I got the balloon down after you nearly crashed it on top of that Garden House—"

"Rubbish!"

"Like when I got us down the ramp here and you were squeaking—"

"I was *not*—"

"You were always a bossy spoiled brat," said Ngarbo.

"And you were always a pain in the ear."

There was something comfortable now about their argument. You could see they were enjoying it, relaxed by it. And it was another scene of an argument that perhaps they had argued all their lives, but only in private. Before others they fought differently, or were distantly polite, or intensely flirted with each other. This was—intimate and personal, this arguing, there in that other dark wood-forest among the other fields of flowers.

I wonder how they *did* manage that ramp—had it been like the one I hadn't chanced? And what had they had for dinner? And Venn and Dengwi too—

I drew back as the blue eyes, foreseeing also what I'd do, closed, and the statue straightened up.

Then I walked off, out of the trees, down to the edge of the river.

I could hear the wolves singing now, proper nontalk wolf yowls. Thu had sat down, frowning like Ngarbo, perhaps thinking now these relatives weren't that like him after all. The moon was going out on the edge of distance.

I wanted so much to look into the last pair of open blue eyes, but I couldn't make myself.

And then, the quietest touch. I thought it was Mirreen come after and nudging me.

I turned. The statue with the black halo-hat had followed, and stood a few inches from me. Its shadow stretched transparent on the grass from starlight. Its body, head, and eyes were bending down and down to where I could reach them.

"Will I see him?"

I took hold of its stone arms and stared in.

He was there. Argul. He rode at walking pace through the night, sitting straight and strong on the horse that matched him. The moon was down, there, and the second ring of true forest looked very near. He hadn't wasted much time.

He had no look of unease, irritation, or anger. Or gentleness.

He was going south. Keeping on. Thinking of and aiming only toward that last confrontation.

With Her.

I couldn't speak. In case he just . . . didn't hear me.

There was room in my husband's thoughts now only for Ustareth, and for her world, and for what she would say when once more he found her. The rest of us—

But all our nerves and squabblings seemed tiny beside this.

Did she keep us two apart, then, because of that? To let him be, with his single-minded quest? To keep me *safe* from it?

The eyes of the statue close, knowing I've seen enough.

Ustareth, the Abandoning Betrayer, the Experimenter and Player of Games.

How can she have made all *this*—and be all *that??*

When I couldn't sleep again, and couldn't see to write, a crowd of fireflies returned and lit up all around. And by their little lamps, I've written this.

WATER AND AIR

For some reason, I feel really great this morning.

As if something exciting and delightful will happen.

Then the stream-river opened a separate hot pool in the bank, just as I was thinking of bathing in it. And the pool water had also a gorgeous scent. I half expected the trees to put out towels, but it isn't necessary in the warm air; I dried in half a minute. And now I, too, smell as enchanting as if I'd used perfumes from Peshamba or Chylomba. Once I was out, the pool shut itself up again, the reeds and lilies sealing over. *They'd* gone, too, in the night, the statues. Gone where? Back to her, I suppose. (What I can't understand at all is how they form out of the air??)

And yes, I've wondered if it's me who was tricked, and that

what their eyes showed me were only somehow pictures—like those picture-butterflies I saw that time in the north. And I don't think it was a trick. I think I was meant to see.

Anyway, now, I think of Argul, and the distance he's covered. I, too, now mean to get on as quickly as I can.

I've ridden fast. We cantered through the meadows, along avenues of trees, Thu leaping at Mirreen's side. Once we all nearly hurtled into a herd of gazelles outside a wood, which only trotted off a short way looking miffed (the gazelles, not the wood). Saw a tiger in the near distance, brilliant orange, lying along the bough of a tree, its tail hanging down. There were monkeys playing in some other trees further on. And I spotted an anteater (brown, long nose) and was pleased I recognized what it was—unless it wasn't. . . .

Have covered miles. Only short rests.

(I was dying for a cup of tea and found a tea-tree. This seemed extra peculiar really. Do the helpful trees somehow read my mind and appear?)

The river—it *is* a river now—still flows with us. The farther bank looks far off. Sometimes I see big fish down there, brightly colored.

And I think, from higher ground, I begin to see the forest wall ahead.

When we stopped in the evening, nothing had happened one way or another, I mean nothing startling. I chose the spot to stop because some trees were walking over, and I thought they might be another Dinner Forest. But in fact, no. Then I considered what we—especially Thu the Ever-Hungry—would eat. But inside five minutes five more trees arrived, and supplied a very good, though much more snacky, supper. I was rather relieved. The other sort of meal is too much every night. (Thu still ate too much.)

Mirreen is thriving on the grass and clover.

As it got dark, I started thinking of the others, as I always do worse when I stop moving. Then, when I went down to the river and took an after-dinner stroll, I found three of the statues, the three I'd looked through last night, sort of waiting for me along the bank. All with open eyes. So, I looked.

"Despite everything, I like this life," said Venn. "I like this walking and traveling on all the time. I was stuck at the Rise so long. My fault—afraid to leave. Afraid of everything."

He hardly seemed to remember *why* he's walking and traveling. Toward Ustareth, his mother.

As if I'd spoken, he added, "I don't say much about *her*, you'll have noticed. I mean Ustareth. What is there to say?"

"But you think about her," said Dengwi. "It seems you must."

"Yes. I hate thinking of her. But as you say, I must."

They were sitting in the flowers, sharing a leaf-plate of apricots and nuts, the shells of which Venn was cracking with his teeth, before handing them to Dengwi like a gentleman.

They look as if they've known each other years.

When he sighs, she rubs his arm once, twice, gentle, with the back of her hand. They sit close.

She likes him, then, after all. He likes her.

It's awful. I feel resentful. Am I envious? Even though . . . It's just—being alone.

I turn away and the blue eyes go out.

As for Winter and Ngarbo—

They're lying on their backs with some wine, laughing and telling each other funny stories, and looking up at the stars. "Look, is that the Empress?" she asks, pointing at a particularly bright lemon star low down. "Power mad, you," he says. And they laugh again, and Winter says, "It's crazy, isn't it, but this isn't bad, is it?" "No, not bad," he says. And I see him smile to himself, which Winter doesn't, craning now after another royally powerful star. (They've rowed so often, it seems, they can throw the rows away at once.)

And again, I turn my head, and the blue eyes close.

I think, They're doing fine.

And again I'm jealous. Because they are together.

While I—

And Argul.

I look at the last statue, standing waiting to show me my best and only love riding alone and grim and forgetful of me through the night, to reach Her faster.

"Thanks, no." And it shuts its eyes.

"Come on, Thu," I say, "let's get on."

I mount up, and we walk, Mirreen, Thu and I, through the swishing grasses, across the soft and cooly whispering starlit night.

Next day in the afternoon, we were charging along. (I'd definitely seen the forest by now. It lay there, black-dark, massive and quite forbidding. [Like a fairy tale forest in a story.] Also, it stretches for miles. Beyond it I couldn't see. Except that faint sketch of something much farther off still, and up in the air, which must be those colossal mountains. Unless clouds really stand still for days here, which maybe they do.)

Anyway, in midcharge, I heard thunder.

And I said to Thu and Mirreen, "So much for the perfect weather."

Then I realized it probably wasn't thunder, because it was going on and on, and getting louder and louder.

I reined in, and turned and looked behind me.

And saw the most utterly terrifying sight.

Perhaps you've noticed, the rivers here aren't normal. A normal river flows out toward the sea. This one (and any others?) flow inward, toward the land's center.

And now, somehow—for there hadn't been any rain I'd seen—this river had turned into a raging torrent. It was so full and rushing, it had come up over the banks and also *stood up in the sky* in a kind of bubbling wave—

It was some way off, but all the time getting closer very fast—and it looked about twelve feet high, that standing-up water—

It was heading straight toward us.

Could we outrun it?

We'd have to.

"Thu—go!" I yelled. And he stared at me in fright, then shot away to the left, running like mad. The ground already rumbling, and there was this electric smell like lightning—and the awful noise and—Mirreen and I plunged after Thu.

And *then*—the real horror—

Like a nightmare.

The lush and flowery grass—it started rearing up in front of us, *growing* before our eyes into high tussocks and tall, tangled clumps, no longer attractive, a jungle. First it slowed us, next it was strangling Mirreen's legs so I thought she'd fall— and Thu actually was falling, all knotted up in the writhing fronds and ghastly ropes of flowers—

We staggered to a halt and I looked and the water was now a wall that looked fifty feet high, veering, roaring toward us so the beaming sky was hidden.

I slid down from Mirreen. I slapped her to make her take off as fast as she could, unhampered by me. I grabbed at Thu and ripped him out of his grass net. I screamed at him again to run—

I said he wasn't very obedient—no, he's loyal—he wouldn't leave me now—barking at the water to scare it off—and anyway, it was hopeless.

Then the river just came.

One minute we were there and then—it was like a huge hand that punched me into the air, turning me over—like the storm that tossed Venn and Winter and Ngarbo—like—it was like nothing I can describe.

I was too frightened to think. I sort of heard and felt and saw this happening to me from far off. And I saw Thu flung up with me, and Mirreen, tossed like a straw. I didn't cry out. My mouth was too full of water. It tasted *fresh* and *clean*. I bathed in it, this enemy, only yesterday—

When I broke through into the open air, I thought (without *thinking*) the strength of the water had simply thrown me a moment up above itself. Then Thu was there with me, and Mirreen came spinning up kicking—and her hoof hit my head—only . . .

Only it didn't.

I hadn't been touched, even though I knew she'd just accidentally brained me—

And we were all floating there, coughing and spitting, in the air.

For a while I just gawped at them, and at the wave of water tearing past below, and trees uprooted and being whirled along by the wave, though that wouldn't matter; once it let go they'd just get up and put down their roots again or walk off somewhere else—

But why were we in the sky?

Why didn't Mirreen hurt me when she *kicked* me in the *head?*

"Thu, here, boy. It's fine. Well done."

Thu turned a somersault not meaning to at all, and looked as if he blamed me for everything. I grabbed his collar. I got hold of Mirreen, too. "There, girl, there, there."

We sailed lazily high above the water, cleared it, came down on a small hill. Mirreen and Thu shook themselves.

I sat down. I thought, *It's the ring—*

I didn't know how, I didn't, right then, care, but somehow the diamond Power ring had recharged itself. It was working again and had saved our lives, lifting not just me but my companions into the air to safety.

Down over there, in the race of water, I saw a huge pearly fish, about the size of a wagon, haring along. Was it this superfish that had caused the boiling tidal wave in the river?

I sit here, drying out, thinking.

I keep looking at my ring.

Ustareth made it, so perhaps being so near her now, the force field itself, which first knocked out the Power, has energized it again.

That seems a silly explanation. And, too, there was no flash of light, not even when the ring saved me from Mirreen's flailing hoof.

It does explain other things, though.

Why the trees seem to come and feed us, rather than us having to find them. Why the statues carried us down to the valleys and now provide me with a way to watch the others.

The ring affected the statues in the first place, and must have drawn them after me. If so, it wasn't, isn't Her.

Although, I wonder if the flood-wave was.

I mean, nothing like that ever happens here. Even the most man-eating animals aren't apparently dangerous. And everything else is *heavenly*. So why a sudden rampaging river that could have killed me?

Does Ustareth in fact want me dead?

The water settled, and sank back in the earth and into the riverbed inside an hour. Fresh flowers came prancing up, pretty and innocent as if they hadn't recently tried to get us all drowned.

Thu and Mirreen seem all right. Thu is still shaking water out of his ears (as I am).

Mirreen eats grass. Yes, eat it before it attacks us again!

Night's coming.

I was going to give us a rest, but I won't sleep.

Even though the ring protects us, I keep thinking *She* made the ring, and may find some way to cancel it again—

Twilight Star tried to kill me. Didn't manage to.

This lady is much more clever and capable than Twilight.

And as the shadows form, so She seems to fill the land with the shadows, Ustareth.

I've decided, since we can, we're going to "fly."

I've practiced with Mirreen. I mounted, then even before I'd pictured us rising, up we went. Not too high, about ten feet off the ground. We stayed together. (The ring responded, just as it always did, to unspoken wishes.)

M was brilliant, a remarkable horse. At first she shied a little, but I kept her steady. Then she got the hang of it. So I took her on a gallop through the air. She sort of swims—she can swim; I saw her doing it in the sea when the Sharkians got us—

So, Mirreen swims through the sky, and I ride on her back, and the rising moon gapes at us in astonishment.

Thu was more difficult.

I kept lifting him up by ring Power, only a couple of feet, and he whined and snarled and kept rolling head-over-heels.

Then it struck me neither Mirreen nor I seem to weigh much in the air. So Thu doesn't either. I got him onto her saddle in front of me, and took us all up that way.

At first he was very unhappy. And then he saw a bird—an owl perhaps—flying by in the night sky.

Thu forgot he didn't like air travel. He was off Mirreen's back, out of my grabbing hands, and away.

"Thu!" I shrieked, "leave it alone!"

But he didn't stop until the owl outflew him into the upper sky. Then I saw him standing there in the air, panting and crestfallen, an odd sight, with a little moon-white cloud passing under his feet.

When I next called to him, he bounded back to me, and sprang up on to Mirreen. Sky? he asked, grinning and thumping his tail. Oh, sky's all right.

I'm impressed.

How long it would have taken to cross the rest of Ustareth's world of Summer I don't know—a month, two months, or more—not this way. Now I can go faster than any of the others—unless of course their Power jewels have also recovered. Yet—I don't think that's happened. Mostly because this ring has always been the most Powerful of all the jewels. Wasn't meant for me, after all, was it, but for Twilight's daughter, Winter Raven, long ago.

Now of course, too, I could go and try to find the others. But what's the point, if they can't do what I'm doing now? Argul, though—no, Argul least of all. I am—I'm afraid to find him, now. He's wrapped up in his Ustareth-quest.

And if I'm honest, She's become my quest, too.

EARTH AND FIRE

We crossed the forest in a night.

In the darkness, *its* darkness expanded. Yet it seemed full of sudden half-seen gleams—like *eyes*—probably water catching the moon.

The trees were huge, pines and firs, and great towering unknown tents of boughs, and other trees like colossal hollyhocks—only black.

Sometimes the treetops brushed Mirreen's hoofs.

Thu stared down (no longer afraid) and once he barked, and from there below (four hundred feet down?) something barked back.

When dawn came, the trees were drawing apart. In their planting, I mean; I hadn't noticed any moving.

Then we were over a rocky landscape, shambles of granite hillsides and ravines, with gorses burning in them like stretches of yellow flame. It was beautiful, this, in its own way. Waterfalls burst from rocks where mists rose like smoke.

Everything was still in vast, curving rings, and this area took most of the day to cross. (Traveling on the ground, it would have taken ages. Would the gorse have produced sandwiches or something?)

Then there was a very large lake, or inland sea.

On it lay islands small as green pebbles.

We saw a whale surface. (I think it was a whale.)

We came down on one of the islands to rest. And there was an orchard of pears and cherries blossoming, and pineapple trees, and they all put out fruit, and some produced fountains of wine, or little sweets, as if to prove we were still in Ustareth-country.

No sails moved on the lake or sea. As no wagons, chariots, carts, or *people* had moved anywhere in this round land. So it was an empty heaven. Except for us (the six of us) and—Her.

It was nice by the lake. The water stayed calm. Didn't come rushing up the shore to get me or anything.

If she had tried that, maybe she'd seen it was useless, at least for now.

I wondered if the statues would appear, but they don't, I think, unless the ring calls them because I really want something they can do. Like looking at the others. And now—I shan't. It's spying, after all. It's what *she* does. Wolf Tower stuff.

I could go on about everything I've seen from the air. The swarm of dragonflies like flying gems. The blue-black bear standing on that hill. It looked as if it were waving to us. Well, *here*, it could have been, couldn't it? So—er, well, I waved back.

Sunset, and the sky and water were fire.

Up here, too, I sort of begin to see properly the effect of circles inside circles . . . but even so, it's still too vast to see the other side—

Beyond the lake, there's a desert!!

I'd realized that she seemed to have put lots of different types of landscape together in this world of hers. And no doubt all partly experimental or changed. Meadows, woods, deep forest, rocky heaths, sea-lake, and miles off what had even looked liked jungles beginning, rising from the lakeshores, those orchid-hung trees and creepery overgrowings, thick with green rain, like at the Rise. But—why a desert? Desert wastes are what she always makes into something else.

We flew on, and the desert went on below, silvery by then in darkness.

When I thought we should take a break we went down, though a desert wasn't the place I felt I'd have chosen to spend part of the night. (And not a dinner tree in sight.)

However.

No sooner were we on the sand than more magical things started to happen. And frankly it was exasperating. Can *nothing* be normally unhelpful here?

Anyway. The sand started to light up softly from within. And by this light, having seen the desert was real sand, not grit and dust, I had to notice the sands were all rainbow colors. Then there came a small sandstorm, buzzing along, only it was, of course, a helpful sandstorm, which circled to our feet, despite Thu's snorting and yacking at it. Then it scattered down and became all sorts of food and drink, tastefully arranged on a sort of glassy tablecloth the sand formed just there. (I think it's the sheer *style* of all this that makes you sick.) But we ate the dinner. There was even some fresh grass for Mirreen.

When the moon had gone over and I'd slept for a while, we went on. Flying as we do, it takes very little effort. And by now I could even get off Mirreen to rest her, and let her swim on alone.

Then, we came straight down again. Because a deep red flash had gone off in the sky to the south, where the land's center is.

It was high, high up. Almost up where the moon had been at its highest. Or so it looked.

Lightning?

Then again. A magenta flash now.

I heard a quiver of sound, so faint as to be more feeling than noise.

We waited on the sand. I was alarmed. Despite the ring, and everything.

But after those two fireworks, nothing else. I waited about half an hour. When we took off again, all was still. As the lit sand again lost its glow, deepest darkness arrived.

And so, though nothing else happened, I didn't keep us up in the sky too long. I was afraid we might run right into— something. Something stuck up high in the air and not light-ing up, except now and then with a scarlet or purple explosion. Also, the desert ended.

Where we next came down was in some hills. They were very gardenlike. Next morning I'd see trees and shrubs either cut or self-growing in ornamental shapes. Smell of roses. The rest of that night, though, we slept.

Most of two days, and part of a night between to cross the garden-hills, even going by air.

This land is vast. How did I see so much from the marble terrace-plateau? Is that some trick, too, some science-magic?

I can see the mountains now.

They are up there, across the hills, and a plain that lies beyond.

I have never seen anything so giant-size. They're—impossible, really. They must touch the sky—or would, if the sky were solid.

They're blue, and at the tops are ghost-white snows. The sun catches them one side at dawn, the other at sunfall, and they flower with red.

Without "flight," how could anyone climb them?

Perhaps no one is meant to.

Well, Ustareth, tough luck.

It's the mountains that breathe fire, despite their snows. They're volcanoes?

Last night we had another brief fireworks display.

Will they *erupt?* That's what volcanoes do, isn't it? Is this her plan, the eruption, to warn me off?

The plain below the volcanoes was smooth, nearly un-marked snow, with healthy leafy trees growing out of it, and other trees that seem to be made *of* snow, with crystal-ice leaves. White foxes run about, and I saw a white bear—which didn't wave.

But I've had enough. I said before I wouldn't say anything else about this place. And look, I've covered pages. No more.

Tomorrow, at first light, we start the flight up the snow-volcanoes. *Can* we get *over* them?

If I'd had any doubts she was there, inside the last ring of mountains, the volcano part has told me she is.

I'm nervous. Didn't even let Thu eat all his chops that the ice-leaf tree, which had joined us, gave him for dinner.

By the way, I have to say this—wouldn't you know it, the snow here is *warm*.

Up the mountains we rose, thousands of feet.

Below, a million tons of rock-stone built in such *crags*. Shelves, rifts, chasms of peacock-blue ice. The long clawings of the cake-icing snow.

And there—a volcanic crater, sulfur-yellow rimmed, a faint glow pulsing in it once, like a sleepy eye—then gone.

Were there birds here? Crows, maybe. No—those straight, unflapping figures weren't birds, blown up on the ice winds as we blew upward. Come from nowhere, as always, the faithful statues from Peshamba that seem to be my ring's servants—but are perhaps truly hers, now followed me to the place beyond the mountain ring. The morning sun gilded their masks, and all their eyes were open.

The air got thin.

I'd expected that, remembering it from high-flying before.

But then a puff of richer air jetted out of somewhere on the nearest mountain. Released, presumably, to help us, or any other visitor.

And then we're up above the snow line, over the carved white and the bottomless drops, where mist stirs like powder. Casting our own tiny shadows.

And so up and over the *crest.*

Hanging in sky, and looking down and in, and there, all that way beneath, was this golden bowl.

It was all gold, gold with emerald. At first I didn't know what it was, but it was things growing, fields of grain, wheat and paler barley, and corn still green, and the spangling of another river like a coiling snake. Normal things, here at the heart of all strangeness. Until a green hill lifted from the fields, one of several, with patterns of trees. But there on this hill, among those trees—

Even so high, I could see *this* thing really was gold, and it was, too, a huge face. A golden face, with wide, dark caves for eyes, staring across the central valley inside the mountains.

We were descending. We'd already dropped some distance.

Now birds did rise—below.

A ribbon of cloud came by, covering and uncovering us, and puffed out more of the richer air, so I realized I'd given up breathing and had better start again.

"Down," I said. "Faster." It was already happening.

We fell like a thunderbolt toward Ustareth's final valley.

THE MASKED PALACE

She's here.

That thought, really just that one, was ringing around and around in my head.

As I rode through the fields of tall gold grain.

(Thu kept to heel; the statues glided after, orderly, in single file, because the paths through the corn were narrow.)

One field gave on another. Now we went through barley.

We reached the fields' edge, natural and unrailed, with a sloping way down to the next lower fields, which were of wheat. That crop was younger, and the stalks were only waist high. I could see this clearly, since someone was walking slowly through the wheat.

The first human figure I've seen in this land, apart from through the eyes of statues.

Long black hair, falling below her knees, I thought. A cream-colored dress tied at the waist with a corn-gold sash. A woman. She wasn't looking up here, not looking my way at all. She was looking at the wheat, feeling, *testing* it, with her slim dark hands.

We took the downslope—stupid, but the ring would protect us—at a gallop. I tore in between the feathery-headed wheat, crushing the stalks with Mirreen's hoofs, Thu tearing alongside.

We pulled up just short of her, clods of soil, the white seed-mist, spraying around us.

She looked up. That was all. Just—looked up at me, still with one hand on the wheat.

"Good morning, Claidi," she said.

It was Her.

When I went with Venn to her house at the village in the jungle, that was when I first saw her. Or, I saw the mechanical doll she'd left him, to be his "Mother" in her place. She'd made the doll exactly like herself, and so, from seeing the doll, I recognized her now. Only, about nineteen, twenty years have passed since she made it.

She's slimmer than then. And her jet black, magnificent (it is) hair has some long white strands in it—just like Mirreen's mane and tail.

Her smoky skin and black eyes—unchanged.

If anything, in a funny way, she looks younger than she did

then. I supposed, standing there, seeing this, dumping everyone as soon as she got tired of them had helped to keep her fit.

Ustareth.

This is Ustareth.

"Good morning, Ustareth," I said. Bitterly I said, "So sorry about trampling your wheat."

"Don't trouble," said Ustareth. "It soon springs up again. Look."

It did.

"You've bred it to do that," I accused.

She smiled.

When she smiled—I could see Argul. Yes, he has a real look of her. Venn, too? I think so.

"It's doing very well," she said of the wheat, as if we were holding an ordinary conversation. "The climate helps, of course."

I said, "You fixed the weather here. Stole it from everywhere else."

"I don't need to do that," she said reasonably. "I simply draw the energy to run everything from all the power sources available. Sun-power, wave-power from the sea, power from the earth itself. And the volcanoes are a prime source. They were here before I was."

"What if they *erupt?*"

"They won't. Now their force is always channeled."

I didn't really understand, only that somehow she can control Everything. Which I'd already known.

Can she control us? Me?

She said, "Let's walk up to my house."

What could I do? I'd come to see her, hadn't I.

"Right," I said.

I swung off Mirreen, and led her, and Thu trotted with us. The statues were still there, too. She made no comment.

As we walked, she just said the occasional thing about the fields, what this crop was, and that one (some were *not* wheat or corn or anything like that). Then we came out on the slope of the hill, and went up through apple orchards and a vineyard. There were a couple of lions sunning themselves on the roof of a shed-building there, but otherwise nothing much peculiar.

She's like a lion herself. I'd thought that before.

Above us, between the lime trees and poplars, the golden mask-head appeared, very large.

"What's that?" I sounded sullen—no, worse, *interested.*

"The house."

"You live inside a golden face."

No comment on that either.

Through the trees was a garden, not formal, wildflowers and white-blossoming trees, some sheep quietly grazing. At a pool, a young woman with a pointy face was standing in the sunlight, who startled me nearly into a shout. But she was more shocked than I was—she flung round and bolted away along the hill.

Ustareth said, "Yes, that was Jade Leaf."

"How did—she *get*—"

"I'll tell you soon," said Ustareth, "when we speak about all the other things."

Just then the golden head on the hilltop did this amazing

trick. Two eyes appeared in the cavelike eye spaces. They were grass green and they blinked, once. Then the whole golden face swung upward and tilted over to become the *roof* of a gleaming, round house. A palace. It had deep blue pillars, standing on a white marble terrace, that opened and led into cool marble rooms beyond, where sun shafts fell like curtains.

A grapevine grew among the pillars.

There was a table there, with a cold jug of lemonade. I could see it. There were two glasses.

"You must be thirsty," she said. "I am."

We sat down on the two chairs, she and I. Ustareth poured the lemonade with her beautiful hand that *made* things. She offered me a plate of cookies and grapes. And I saw the plate wasn't glassy or gold—it was old and chipped, with a faded, glorious design. A Peshamban plate.

Down the hill, the thirteen statues had stopped in their neatest line. Their eyes had shut now.

Thu hadn't come up, even for the cookies. He was sitting there watching us, by the dark blue–robed female statue he seems to prefer. Mirreen, hitched to the post Ustareth had shown me, was quietly nibbling the grass like the sheep.

"Am I the only one here?" I said. "I mean apart from *Jade Leaf.*"

"Yes. The first to arrive."

I felt I knew her. It's because of Argul. But it made things more awkward. I wanted to hate her. I needed to be wary.

"Claidi," she said. (Of course, since she *watches* everyone, she knows the value of calling me by the only name I can accept as mine.) "Shall I tell you everything now?"

"Tell me first why you left Argul and his father."

"Ah," she said.

I said, "Abandoning Venn when he was *two* I understood, though I think you were scum to do it. They'd forced you to do what the Towers wanted. You felt you had to rebel, to escape. But *Argul?* You said you loved his father. You even took a Hulta name. Argul thought you loved *him.* Why?"

"Oh, Claidi," she said. She sighed.

She had no right to *sigh.*

"No reason then, you just got bored—"

She held up her hand.

It really was a wonderful hand. Calloused from working in fields and orchards despite all the clever machines she must have here. A working hand, graceful from use. And it was, too, the hand of a great woman, a Ruler. Not royalty—but real *true* importance. The kind that has nothing to do with anything but the person who has it.

So when she did that, I couldn't say anything.

Instead I glared, and gulped the lemonade.

"Claidi, I agree that leaving Venn was unforgivable. He never will ever forgive me, nor would I expect him to. Yes, I felt everything you said. That I must escape the Law and the rule of the Towers. But I could have taken my little son *with* me, couldn't I? I didn't. I was a young woman, not much older than you are now, and I felt I was a slave. You'll know very well what I mean. This isn't an excuse for what I did. Only the reason."

"All right. But then you were free and with the Hulta—so why leave *Argul*—"

Her eyes held mine. She has thinking eyes—no, dreamer's. But she can make the dreams real.

"Why would you think?" she said. "What possible reason could I have had?"

"You told them you were ill and you'd die. Then you tricked them somehow. I don't know how, if it wasn't one of your *dolls* they buried—"

She said simply, "It was a medicine I knew how to make. I took that, and it made me seem for some while to be dead. I left careful instructions for the burial. The Hulta obeyed them. I had them put one of my mechanical servants, a very little creature, with me into the grave. Once I came to, it tunneled a route out for me under the ground. I emerged quite a distance away. The grave site wasn't even disturbed."

"Awfully clever."

Her eyes after all flashed—a flare of temper, like her volcanoes. But then she shook her head and was calm. And again, that's like Argul, her self-control.

"Yes, I am clever. But Claidi, why do you think I went to so much effort to convince them all I'd died? Just to make an easy getaway?"

"I haven't a clue."

"Haven't you?"

"You'll say for some reason you had no choice."

The sheep bleated. I saw the two lions were swaggering up from the orchard, the sheep running over and butting at them. Old friends.

Ustareth folded her hands together.

"I shall tell you," she said again, "everything."

"My first husband, Narsident, was a cruel and disgusting man. I won't say much about him. He deserves no words of mine. To my pleasure, I see nothing of him in Venarion—Venn. Except, perhaps, Venn's irritable side.

"I did what I was sent to do at the Rise, and in the wasteland to which the Towers—the Wolf Tower—had exiled me. It was their mockery, really. As they said, I'd taught myself science, and could *make things grow.* Since I wouldn't obey them at home, I could go and try that, see if I could. They expected me to fail. I didn't. I succeeded." (Remembered triumph lit her face.) *"Didn't* I! And then—I just ran away. I tried to leave Venn someone to care for him. But I was so impatient to go, so selfish. I hadn't had much chance to be, before then.

"When I met Argul's father—don't you know his name? He was called Kirad—when I met Kirad, I was in love. You know what that's like. He was like Argul. You see? Very like him. The strength and honor in that man, how he cared for his people— I was so happy, Claidi. And I did everything I could to serve the Hulta, too. I developed my skills as a healer, setting broken bones perfectly, making salves for wounds and bruises that could cure swiftly and leave no scar. And for many illnesses, too, I made cures. They got used to me, to my machines—although I let them see very few of those. I hid so much of what I could do—oh, even from my husband. I didn't want to burden them with all that. Or frighten them—I was afraid they'd stop liking me. They called me the Magician anyway.

"When Argul arrived, that was the second great happiness. Poor Venn—after his father, it was difficult for me to love him.

But then, I never really tried. With Argul I didn't have to try. From the first, he was mine, mine and Kirad's.

"So then why did I go?

"You know that I was still experimenting, learning, testing everything. Not the Hulta—I didn't abuse their trust. You know, too, that I visited Ironel, my mother, and Twilight Star in her winter country. Sometimes I needed that companionship, women who knew me as I *was*. I was a friend to Twilight. But finally I saw her as a fool. Why else have I never told her I'm alive, and here? She was a woman of the Towers, and still is. Ritual, royalty, rules, playing with people. You think that I do that. But if I did, never as Twilight would like to. Her values—are absurd. That plan to create a super-human—a Wolf Queen—and she told you it was my plan, too. Claidi, in my mind, it was something I'd thought about, not as something to cause, but something that might happen on its own. Naturally."

I spoke. "Just as it's all so natural, isn't it, *here*. The trees making food, the animals not needing to hunt—"

"Here," she said sharply, "*that* is natural. Yes. Do you prefer the other system? Starving for want of food, and a tiger that kills and eats a deer, and next you? Yes, I like the fact that doesn't happen here. That if I see an animal racing along, it's doing it because it likes to, not because it *must*. Think of it, perhaps, as another Broken Law. Animals aren't people, Claidi. That's why one must be more sensitive and courteous in their treatment. They're another race—many races—and we don't speak their language."

"What about the sharks?" I cried.

"Let me come to that," she said. "For now, I'll only say, I don't *play* with—or *experiment on* or *breed* human things, even for their own good. Now, let me continue.

"I was with the Hulta, and happy. Then one day, I learned something new. And this was about myself." She paused. She looked away from me for the first time, as if ashamed. She said, "I learned I'd become ill, with a disease which would end my life, horribly and quite swiftly. *I*, the Clever One.

"Listen to me carefully, and try to believe now what I say. You know what I can do—Ustareth-Zeera, the Scientist-Magician. Was it arrogance? Perhaps. I thought I might be able to cure myself, although I knew very well my illness was reckoned *in*curable, and there was no one else in the world who could. But nor could I work the cure if I stayed among the Hulta. It would be impossible to do what I must there. Because the cure I and my machines developed, though it alone might be successful, was almost more terrible than the disease itself."

We sat in silence, under the mountains.

(Thu had lain down, and slept.)

"Besides, if this awful cure didn't succeed, I would still die. That, too, made me sure I must go away at once. I didn't want Kirad to see my struggle, perhaps see me lose it—let alone Argul, who was still a child. I thought, Since I may well die anyway, I shall *pretend* to die now. Then they're free of all this horror, and I can fight with it alone, and better. That then was what I did."

Another long silence.

"Your cure worked," I said.

"Yes. As you see. It was an ordeal I'd wish on no one—but I wanted to live."

I burst out, "But if you were cured, why didn't you go back to them *then?*"

"Claidi—I had to be sure I *was* cured. The disease was such, I couldn't be certain for a great while—years—that I was safe. What was I to do? Return from the dead to Kirad, only to die in front of him again? No. I kept myself from them. I worked alone. I found and came to this barren continent, empty of almost anything. A blank canvas. I made it into what it is now. And by the time I'd finished, I knew too that I was whole and would survive. And by then also, of course, I knew that my husband was dead, my son an adult, and the Hulta leader. And I had no place there anymore."

"You'd *watched* them," I said. "How else *could* you know all that?"

"Claidi, I think you, too, if you'd been able, would have watched them in my circumstances. They were my family. My husband and my son."

I went red. *Did* I believe her—about any of it? Yes . . . No?

As if I'd said this, she added, "Try also to believe *this*—now is the first time I've had the courage to call my sons back to me. And that, Claidi, in a way, is because of you."

So now, the rest of her story, her words to me.

She said she left the diamond ring and the "charm" for Argul. So he could be sure the woman he wanted most—that he and she were right for each other. Ustareth told me that wasn't because she meant it to be Winter Raven. Apparently that was

Twilight's idea. Ustareth said that she had thought quite early on that Argul had a certain "natural" gift which neither she, nor his father, had had. "If that were so, Claidi, then the woman he spent his life with might need to have it also. And it was that the 'charm' showed him, your natural ability. Yes, even more than the chemistry of your being right for him and he for you."

I was offended by that. The "charm" then hadn't shown love? It showed—Natural Ability—what did she mean? But she was going on.

The diamond, she said, was to help the woman Argul married. It would give great powers, but only to one who could use it.

"When you first came to the Wolf Tower, Claidi, things happened that forced you again and again toward this truth. When Nemian tagged your diary—yes, it was Nemian—so you could be found and caught again—and when Ironel sent you off to the Rise to save you from the Wolf Tower—you got pushed into a nearness with the things that had been mine. It seems you always have been. Which was all chance. Certainly I didn't make it happen. But Claidi, as my mother once told you, chance also plays with our lives."

She said I'd grown better and better at being "in tune" with the Power ring. This ring wasn't like the Power jewels Twilight had made, not even like the sapphire Ironel gave to Argul, and that he added to the "charm" to charge it. I'd quickly discovered the diamond was stronger.

"No," said Ustareth. "What's stronger is you."

I sat scowling. The sun stood high above the central valley. It was very quiet, though I could hear the hum of bees.

"Me."

"The Power jewels," said Ustareth, "when worn, give people abilities they don't actually have. For example, what you call flight. *Your* ring—yes, now truly yours—isn't the same. This ring, if often worn, teaches your *own* powers how to work."

I stared. "What are my *own powers?*"

"I can't show you," she said. "You must show yourself. Take off the ring."

"No," I said. I looked at it. The sun blazed in the diamond. *"No."*

"Take it off," she said again. Now it was her other voice, that of command.

I thought, So what. I thought, To all the rest, this is nothing.

So I took off the ring, which had meant so much, and perhaps, like the "charm," had nothing to do with what it meant. It lay there on the table, turned so the sun no longer shone in it.

"Claidi," said Ustareth, gently, "just fly."

"Don't be—" I said.

But when she'd spoken the words, my memory of flying came, and

and

She has done this. Another trick—

No. It's me.

Thu raised his nose, wrinkled his brows, and glanced at me

as I swooped over his head. I landed light as wheat pollen on the grass by the statues.

"You did it when the river boiled," she said. "*You* did it. And you lifted your dog and your horse clear of the water with you. You were in a panic, not even able to think—and you *did* it. No Power jewel has the strength to lift more than its wearer, Claidi—remember other times . . . even then, it was beginning to be you, not the ring. In any case, the diamond lost all its Power, as did the other jewels, and Yinyay, the moment you all came down in the sea."

I said nothing.

"And yes, I sent the river after you," she said. "Lose your temper if you want, but don't be too angry. I already knew, from what you'd already done, it wouldn't be much of a problem."

"I could have drowned!"

"I doubted that. And see, I was right."

"And if you'd been wrong—"

"I could have saved you. Your animals, too."

"Oh yes."

"Yes."

"So it was a *test*—" I blabbled.

"Indeed. And how you passed my test. All my tests. Argul has psychic ability, Claidi. But not like yours. Few have. The ring's done its work with you and woken up your own powers, which were always there inside you. So don't be afraid of me; don't even bother to hate me. To you, now, I'm what the Hulta say, 'A candleflame to the sun.'"

My legs felt unleglike, and I sat down cautiously by Thu,

who licked my hand very thoroughly, in case there was any cookie left there.

I'm sitting up now on another hill in Her Valley, with olive trees. I flew up. It's, well, second nature to me, flying. Easy. Unlike everything else.

The sun's gone over. Shadows getting longer. There's a gap (arranged?) in the mountains to the west, just right to show off the sunsets.

She told me everything, as she said.

She told me everything I'd done, and not known I had, thinking it was the ring—or her—or someone else. Never, never—me.

Why would I think it was ME? *I'm*—me.

On the shark ship, we were all separated—especially Argul and I (she said) to see what we'd be able to do, minus the Power jewels. For example, if we could speak to each other in our heads—telepathically! Well, I hadn't managed *that*. Meanwhile, apparently, no one but the Sharkians could work their lifts—but I did, even if not very accurately. Almost nobody else understood the Sharkians either—but somehow I did understand their speech, or some of it. (She said Argul was not bad at understanding them. Probably because he has another Natural Ability with languages.) The shark boat, when it put me off at the shore, was meant to get us all out instantly, turn us out into the sea if we wouldn't leave. But I'd kept it there and it hadn't been able to, and the shuddering it had gone into had been the boat trying to *resist* what I (not knowing anything about it) was doing to it.

Then I opened the door through the wall.

She said Argul, too, managed to open one of these doors. With the others, *she'd* had to open the doors for them.

(She's watched us all this while, of course. But I knew that. Maybe she's even watching me now. Or can I, now, somehow *stop* that?)

She said yes, the food trees would help anyone, but they'd come *walking toward* me, instead of my having to find them. Even fireflies came to give me light to write in this book.

"I knew," she said, "when I gave you the statues, at Peshamba."

Dully I said, "You gave me the statues."

"They were mine. As you've long known, I helped create Peshamba. And the statues were another of my—what you would call—games. Certain people have always been able to make them move a little. But as they look very like some of the other dolls scattered around parts of the town, no one worried too much if they were seen in motion. But no one has ever been able to make them move about as you did. You and the ring combined, first to make them appear—they hadn't been seen in the Mask Grove for some while—and then you shifted them right out on the street. When they followed you, they weren't chasing you, Claidi. They'd become your servants."

"I'm—I was a servant."

"Yes. So from your own experience, don't you think it's far better to have servants made of stone and metal, who really don't *mind* serving?"

The statues are my servants, then. They kept appearing when I got in a state—but I hadn't, as she put it, yet *mastered* them—and I was nervous of them, too. So they'd appear and then vanish. Not until I was here, and wouldn't risk the ramp, and they flew me down to the meadows, did I really get them working.

"Where do they appear *from?*" I said.

"Out of the air, quite literally," she told me. She then explained, and of *course* I haven't the faintest what she meant. She said they form by changing "matter" and "molecules" (Yinyay used to go on about molecules) and *integrate*, then they are taken apart again (?) and *dis*-integrate, and vanish.

"I have my own mechanical servants here, which also do this. They look very similar to the ones that are now yours. In fact, when you were at the House this time, and saw two of these figures in the grounds there, they were my servants that you saw, not your own. However, even these became visible—integrated—because of your own Power, and that of your ring. You probably wonder why I sent my mechanicals there—I'm afraid it was to conduct an experiment, and on a human thing—just as you always think I must be doing, and generally I am not. Although, you may not think, in this case, she *is* human."

I stared. Then I said, "You *disintegrated* Jade Leaf—and had her brought here."

"Yes. One does this by grasping hold of the mechanical statues, who are able to come and go that way themselves. They take you with them, and return you where they're told. This time they took hold of Jade Leaf, not the other way about, of course. I'm sure you're very shocked. But it doesn't hurt, moving in that way. Disintegration is a pleasant, airy sensation. You see, I've done it myself a number of times. One can then cover vast distances—it really is the fastest of all methods of travel."

I shook my head, as Thu does to clear his ears of water. "Why did you want her?" I asked.

Was I feeling *protective* of Jade Leaf?

Ustareth shrugged slightly, a little impatient again.

"I said, an experiment."

And there we have it, don't we. The Experiment, Science and Knowing, come first. But then she added, "I might make something of her, with time. She's a wretched little thing. Perhaps she can be changed."

And so, *another* experiment.

"Great," I said.

And she just nodded. She said, "She's been a little upset, inevitably."

Poor old Jade Leaf. I mean she's foul and it serves her right and all that. But—one minute there in the Garden of the House, happily trying to stab Dengwi and me in the back, then flung away by the ring (or by some Power of *mine??*) and next gripped by a stone figure, disintegrated and reintegrated here, to be *changed*.

(I've seen her again, JL, in fact, down in the fields. She was wandering along picking cornflowers and poppies, and singing a little song to herself. I couldn't hear the words, but she probably made it up and so it'll be a load of twag. Still, she's been dis- and re-integrated. And not changed yet. That's nearly a relief.) (Her hair's growing back.)

What else did Ustareth say to me? So much. I'm trying to

remember and put it all down (as if I could EVER forget).

But, I sort of do forget, really. I mean—*me?*

She said I'm the Powerful one. And—it seems I am. She says it doesn't make any difference who you are or where you're born—king, queen, servant, slave, educated, un—this kind of Power just comes. Though it may, if it's in a child, be in their sister or brother. Venn, though, she says, doesn't have much of this Power at all, even though Argul is "gifted." Winter and Ngarbo, as she suspected (as *I* did, too), have none. Frankly I think she merely let them come along for the ride. "What about Dengwi?" I asked. "I hold," said Ustareth, "some great hopes for Dengwi."

She says I can call Yinyay. I'll be able to do it. She says it's probably the only way the others will ever get here, if Yinyay is brought up from the ocean, recharged and made large again, and sent to fetch them. And all this—by me.

Ustareth said, actually *smirking*, "And I can't do it, Claidi. Yinyay doesn't recognize me anymore. Remember, Venn ordered all memory of me wiped from her mechanisms." (Ustareth, as I do, calls Yin "she." She thanks her machines, as well. "Thank you," she said when they served us lunch. Was she always like that? In her own diary at the Rise, she seemed more abrasive and in a hurry. But I suppose she's over that now. As she's over wanting to make rooms move about, or crossing rabbits with tigers. She survived death, and she's free.)

She wants Argul, though, and Venn. She does. I can see it in her face when she speaks about them. Aside from all this Power stuff, she talked endlessly through lunch about how they were when they were children. Even Venn. She *confided* in me.

I keep seeing her in my mind, not as she is now, but back before. I keep seeing her leaving the Rise, angry, refusing to look over her shoulder. And I see her, too, gaunt and grey with the illness and its "frightful cure," before it worked, looking through some statue with eyes at her husband, Kirad, and her son, Argul. Looking and looking as if she had to memorize them. And they never knew.

She says I made the eyes open in "my" statues. And it was my Power that made me able even to be heard by the others— if I'd wanted. "You could have appeared to them," she said.

I'd never do that! Scare the life out of them.

That's why she never "appeared" to Argul or his father, I suppose.

And when she could have gone back, Kirad was dead, and Argul was a man.

Do I feel sorry for Ustareth? Do I trust and believe her? Are we convinced, you and I?

She says the Sharkians are one of several Animal Races she has "enabled to develop" humanly recognizable speech, and various other human abilities. She says they might get these things themselves very likely, anyway, in a few million years. She's just hurried things up a bit. She told me there were monkeys in another place, beyond this continent, a Monkey Tower. And Bears somewhere, and Rats and Dogs—possibly there are lots more. She's kept busy.

I don't know what I think of that. Of any of it.

She has, despite anything she may say, experimented on *me!*

She said she knew I'd been the substitute for Twilight and Fengrey's daughter, at the House. Then, when I met Argul, at whom she's gone on looking, from time to time, she took an interest in me. She didn't/doesn't interfere, she said. Only ever watches. (Worse, perhaps?)

"You've always had a psychic knack," she announced. She reminded me about when I was a maid and I'd wished a swarm of bees on Jade Leaf. "What she got was a swarm of ants, but it wasn't a bad try."

So in spite of what she said, she was watching me even then, wasn't she.

The thing about the ants is true, though. At the time I'd thought—well, I hadn't really thought.

She said I sensed, psychically, that Argul had been driven apart from me, when I was taken to the Rise. That's also true. It's like the way Venn and Argul suddenly sensed that Ustareth was alive. *I* didn't. I didn't want to, did I?

She remarked to me, "And now you have an important choice, Claidi. When you see Argul again, will you risk telling him how Powerful you really are now? Or will you lie, as I did to Kirad? Put the ring back on and say it's only that? I wonder what you'll decide."

But I think, when Argul gets here, all he's going to be interested in—is HER.

So. Shall I call Yinyay—see if I can? I'm not wearing the ring. Then bring everyone to her unmasked palace in the sunset?

Or only go on watching the shadows lengthen over the yellow corn?

OURS

Argul rode across the mountains about half an hour later. He rode through the air. His horse swam the way Mirreen does, when she "flies."

He must have seen the golden-topped building on the hill, as I had, when it had a golden face. But I was jumping about on the other hill, waving frantically, and somehow he saw me better. Perhaps I can make people see me, now.

They landed faultlessly.

Then he was there, and lifting me up off my feet.

For a time we didn't say a word, just held each other. After all, he hadn't quite forgotten me.

"We have to stop getting separated like this, Claidi. It's getting to be a bad habit."

"Yes. But she meant us to be."

"I know that. Is she here?"

So I'm to be the one to tell him.

"She's over there, in that palace with the gold roof."

We looked at the palace.

"You've met her," he said.

"Yes—"

"There's a lot to tell me, is there? There usually is."

I took a breath. "I can tell you, or I can wait until—I don't know which will be best."

I wondered then if she had confided in me, in the hopes I might make excuses for her to him. Rather than annoy me, it seemed really sad, that. Like my image of her staring at him through the statue-eyes. This Powerful mysterious woman, helpless and unsure.

But he said, "Don't say anything about her yet. It's best I hear it from her."

His face was set. Waiting for her. (Shall I always see her in his face, now, always see his face in hers?)

"Yes," I said, "go and find her. Fly there—" I hesitated. One thing I did want him to hear now and *not* from her, "Only, Argul, it isn't the Power coming back in the sapphire—"

"I know," he said. He grinned. "How could it be, here? I tried it out, just me, then with the horse—flying. I began to think something was going on when all those trees were rushing up with hot food." (And I thought, whatever Gift I have, I don't have one for being quick on the uptake, do I? He worked out what he could do. I had to be thrown in a river and *shown*.

And I imagined Ustareth making the river boil and chase me, not with a nasty, cruel leer, but tapping her fingers from impatience at my slowness!) Argul said, "So if I've learned how to do this, somehow—are you the same?"

I nodded.

Even she had thought this might be a problem, telling him. Oh, there is more to tell—but already he has some idea. Things often get more simple, when he's with me.

He kissed me, and the breeze turned over all the silver leaves of the olive trees. My husband walked away down the hill to meet his mother.

Yinyay brought everyone else. Yes, I called her, and it worked. Her Power returned, she grew large, there in the sea—and soon she too *blew* up over the mountain crags like a white pillar of cloud.

When she'd parked on my hill, there was thunderous barking and up raced Thu from the fields below. He greeted the many storeys of Yinyay with roars of delight, bouncing at her doors, and then tumbling inside when she opened them. He then shot off up the nearest stairway, and straight into the first lift. Soon his pleased bellows echoed down from the bone-burying lawn.

I tried to get him out before she took off to find the others. Thu wouldn't leave. So Yinyay is the one he really loves and feels loyal to. Constant biscuit-feeding has its uses.

I didn't go with her. Venn and the rest know her by now, the Human Tower (U's palace, too, has a human face). And Yin will explain to them. Really, I can't deal with them just yet.

I think to myself, If Argul found he had Powers, why didn't he try to find me? If I'd known earlier, I would have—or would I? No, I'd have left him alone, once I saw how he was, and that he was all right. Well, I *did* leave him alone. And then I think, Did he find some way to *look at me???*

I'll go down in a little while, and then up to the garden again. About an hour to sunset. Argul has been gone a long while. With her.

And she knows, doesn't she, I can call one of my stone servants(!) and instantly see and hear what she and Argul say to each other. If I'm as Powerful as she says, even she can't stop me.

Therefore I won't. I will never ever do any of that unless I have to.

The sun set perfectly, framed in the artistic gap in the mountains. (She said the mountains were here from the start, so maybe God arranged the view.)

I was sitting by the pool by then. And Yinyay had again come back. Winter and Ngarbo were strutting about the wildflower lawns, eating apples from Her orchard (this was all a holiday to them?), pure Raven Tower stuck-up sightseers. Even disapproving—Winter: "It's quite *small* for a palace, don't you think?"

Dengwi sat under a magnolia tree, silent. Venn, too, had gone inside without a word.

Now and then Dengwi and I glanced at each other.

We didn't mutter, What is she *saying* to them? How are they *dealing* with it?

From Yinyay down in the orchards, Thu's barks sometimes trumpeted back to us. Swallows were darting over the sky.

"It's all a bit village-y really, isn't it, Claid?" said Winter.

"Not like Chylomba."

"God, no," said Winter. Then, "I suppose *I'll* have to meet her, too. She was Mother's best friend, after all. Only good manners." She'd know all about those.

Ngarbo looked at my face, and drew Winter off again. Soon they were doing some sort of dance under the apple trees below, stared at by sheep.

The sunset got redder, and everything was red, and a red stone statue came gliding out of the palace.

Was the statue one of mine—or hers? Mine. Now I knew—I knew.

It didn't speak but its eyes opened—and—*I heard what it said.* That is, I heard it in my head. (Am I becoming telepathic, then, as she's expected me to all along?)

Another shock. It's all shocks.

I walked over to Dengwi. "She wants us to go in."

Dengwi didn't say, How do you know? She stood up, and together we walked up the marble step onto the terrace. Only Ngarbo in the orchard saw us. Somehow he kept Winter dancing with her back to us so she didn't, until it was too late. He's all right, Ngarbo.

The swallows, who can fly all night on the summery updrafts, were passing like scores of dark blue bows and arrows, across the wide-open windows of Ustareth's Hall. Now and then one or two flew inside, and for a moment gripped the pillar tops with their claws, before making off again. They don't really have legs—just wings and claws. In the sky so much, they don't need legs, so they've gradually lost them.

When I go from this place, me, this Powerful One who can also fly, let me remember always the swallows, and not lose my ability to walk with my feet on the ground.

Venn came slamming out as we got to the doorway. He did this though the doorway was wide and doorless.

There was a storm in his white face.

Seeing Dengwi and me, he stopped. He said, "Claidi, I'm sorry—I can't, now." Whatever that meant. Then he came up to Dengwi and stood there staring into her face. She put her hands up to his shoulders and he kissed her on the mouth. Then he left us, strode away, down the marble spaces of the palace.

I wasn't, by now, amazed at the kiss. It had been very obvious, from how I'd seen them before, they weren't enemies, or even just-friends anymore.

But Dengwi said, "He told me he could never forgive her. He hasn't. He never will."

"No," I said. "She didn't think he would, either."

"It's as if his anger at her is all that holds him together—let go of it, he'll break apart." But she spoke calmly. She said, "For now."

Then we crossed the threshold.

I'd expected Argul to be there, but he wasn't. Only Usta-reth was.

I had this sudden uneasy memory of what Argul told me,

how she'd called everyone in to see her, one by one, when she was "dying."

She certainly looked drained, older than at lunchtime. But she stood and waited for us.

Then she said, "It's done. How I've dreaded it. But it's over. They're yours now, my sons, no longer mine. Yours."

That was all—*all*. After it she turned to Dengwi, and Ustareth said, "Tell Claidi what you know. Tell her now."

And then—she just went away.

I stood there in the fading light, and the arrivals and departures of the swallows.

"Tell me *what?* What *now?*"

Dengwi looked at me. She said, "She seems to know everything. Does she know this—the right moment to tell you—"

"If you don't, I may pick up that marble vase over there and—"

"All right. Here it is then. That night of the lions, when you escaped with Nemian—Jizania told me that night. When you came back to the House, I wanted to tell you—but, as I say, I wanted to choose the right moment. Then Jizania again—announcing to everyone Lorio was my father. Perhaps he was. I'll never know. But it stopped me anyway, stopped me speaking to you as I meant. Now—well, does Lorio even matter now? *We* matter."

I looked at her, and I was almost frightened—only it wasn't fear—

"Claidi," she said, "my mother was a slave."

"Mine too," I said, because she paused. "Not that I know who she was."

Dengwi nodded. "I know you don't. But I did know my mother a while. She said she'd had two children, but by different fathers. I came from the 'special' father [Lorio?] but the other kid's father was a slave like mum."

"I remember you spoke to me once about your sister. You said she'd been whipped and almost died."

"Sorry, Claidi. I was lying then. I wanted to make you really fight against being whipped, because I thought you had a chance—and I was right. No, at that time I believed my sister had never been old enough to be whipped. Mum had said she died soon after she was born. But then, when I was with Jizania that night, before the rebellion—she told me my *mother* was the one who'd been lying. My mother was forced to lie—to say her first baby died. Jizania knew for sure, because she was the one who forced Mum to do it. And why? Jizania had wanted that child to take the place of another one, a royal one. Twilight's child by Fengrey."

I, the Powerful One, stood as I always do in the end, mouth dropped open.

I couldn't even ask. Dengwi said it anyway.

"My mother's other child, the one born the year before I was—was you. We're sisters. Half-sisters. Is that enough?"

That, then, is why Ustareth wanted to bring Dengwi here, make her go through all the tests too, see if, like me, she has this Power. And U "holds great hopes" for Dengwi.

Well, so do I. Probably not the same ones.

I'm shy of her, though. Really *shy*. She, too?

No wonder she wanted to wait to tell me.

Jizania—oh, that meddling Old Woman.

(I know from Dengwi, too, why Jizania hates Jade Leaf. Seems the ever-faithful love-match of Twilight and Fengrey— wasn't, quite. Jade Leaf is his other daughter—and not by Twilight, of course, but that other princess called Shimra, Twilight's great friend! Oh, it's typical.)

We walked about in the darkening dusk Hall. It's very grand, the Hall. When Winter sees it, she'll approve.

D and I didn't say much. A tiny bit about her—*our*— mother—but she scarcely remembers her—and it sounds so awful and wickedly sad—so we left that really for another time. And then we murmured things like, The swallows are extraordinary, aren't they?

Eventually, "You don't mind about Venn?" she said.

"You and him? Oh, no."

I *knew*, Dengwi, I knew even before the two of you quite did, spying on you, not meaning to—

"Perhaps," she said generously, "he sees something of you in me."

"Perhaps," I said, "he just really likes you and has fallen for you—and needs you, especially now. You like *him?*"

She smiled. "Mmm. I do."

From a window, we saw Ngarbo and Winter furiously rowing on the lawn. Enjoying doing it very much. Will Winter feel she has to pretend she's jealous of Dengwi now?

But, "Oh, look—Ngarbo's kissing her," said Dengwi as we craned from the window. "Probably the only way," I suggested, "to shut her up."

All this love, these kisses, making up—something in the air?

Only not for everyone. Not for Ustareth. Venn. Argul?

But D and I are giggling as we spy *openly* through the window on N and W. For a minute we're—sisters. Feel that. Start back scared. We'll have to learn this one.

And Venn and Argul meanwhile, She has graciously given them to us (like in the Hulta marriage ceremony, where the Old Man and Old Woman marry the groom to the bride, the bride to the groom). They're Ours.

We must keep them safe.

Supper appeared on a table in a wide room. Lamps had been lit, the usual Ustareth light that comes on its own and doesn't flicker. We wandered in and out, picking at the food.

Outside the windows, one of the volcanoes had a little light show that *did* flicker quite a bit, but not for long.

There's an astRolabe in this room. I remember the other one, with Venn. I know how to spell it now.

Venn appeared, took me aside. He apologized to me for saying he was still after me, when we were all on the way here, and then apologized for *not* being after me anymore.

"Changing partners," I said. I thought of how I'd been over Nemian, and then found Argul. I'm not going to think at all about when I was with Venn at the Rise and felt so close to him. And I'm not jealous of Dengwi. That was just something stupid, fleeting. I *like* the way they are. (I only wish Venn and Argul could get to know each other—but I can sense, well, I can *see* that's not going to happen.)

Anyway, after all this, Venn didn't know what else to say to me, so I rescued him by mentioning Dengwi—and then he found *everything* to say; *stopping* him was much harder.

Ustareth didn't come to eat. Nor did Argul. I'd put on the diamond ring again. I'd put on a really good dress he likes that Yinyay made me ages ago.

I got nervous, and in the end I went out onto the terrace, and there he was, coming up through the orchard. So, I went down to meet him.

My friend, if you're still reading this, let me say I'm sorry, too, for not being able to tell you, after all *this*, what Venn and Ustareth said to each other, or what Argul and Ustareth said. I wouldn't spy on them, and neither of them has told me anything, really, beyond what's obvious. So I don't know. I hope you'll understand. Please do.

"Beautiful evening," said Argul.

"Yes."

I took his arm, and we walked in the orchard, between the trees and the wooly boulders of resting sheep, under the stars.

"I'm going back, Claidi," he said, "to my—to our people, to the Hulta. I know what I said, but that's changed. Will you mind that, going back? I know they gave you a rough time when they believed all that Wolf Tower rubbish about you— we'll put them right. They should know the mistake they made about you. You're nodding."

"Yes, I don't mind if we go back."

"*Good.* I may not be needed as leader now; even so, I'll get something to do. Hulta don't waste things or people. Is that all right as well?"

After I'd told him again it was, he said, "This is because of her, really. She wouldn't risk going back, and I haven't. She could have taken the chance. I can, and I'm going to. What did she think we'd do to her?"

Later, he said, "I've *forgiven* her. That's a strange way of putting it—her way. I believe what she told me about why she left us. It's *like* her. The kind part is, by telling me, she's given me back the mother I had, the one who was wonderful, and that I didn't lose when she died, not completely, but totally lost when all this came up, and I knew she'd lied to us all, to my father, and to me. You think, was it all a lie then? But no, it wasn't. And I've got Zeera back again, in my past. But. I don't know this one, now. This one is *Ustareth*. She looks like my mother could look, acts like her. But she's nothing to do with me."

And later again, when I'd told him about Dengwi and me, he said Dengwi must come to our wedding. "Yes, Claidi, because we'll get married again, in Hulta style. You in a green and white dress riding your bride-horse. We'll do it right, the way it should have been." (Can you get married to the same person twice? Well, I don't see why not.) He says he saw at once the likeness between Dengwi and me. "More in the way you do certain things, your expressions." Can this be true?

Argul and I went back down the slope to Yinyay, and even later than that, I took out Dagger's gift to me, her Hulta dagger, and laid it across the pretty Peshamban marriage certificate, like a promise.

WOLF WING

Next morning, Jade Leaf came to the door of Yinyay.

There she was.

"Well," she said, screwing up her face at me. For a minute, you could see, she was back in the old jolly days when she could scream at and beat me and have me whipped to death. Then it all came home to her, poor thing, how nothing was like that anymore. And—that she was afraid of me. She wilted. "Uss—Ustareth s-says . . . will you please come up to the house, please."

She's the maid—the slave.

I'm the Lady.

She means nothing anymore.

We went up to the house.

Ustareth was sitting in her own library, which is small but packed with books and objects.

"Before you leave, and I know, of course, you're all leaving—if I hadn't, Winter has graciously told me—I wanted to speak to you one more time. No, not to everyone else. Only you, Claidi."

I braced myself for one further test. But in a way, it was difficult to be standoffish. I'd seen all through her for a little while; she'd let me. And now I could see how she blossomed when I was there. She likes me, likes being with me. Of course I know *why*. I—and Dengwi—are the closest she can get now, to her sons. (Which may explain why she paired them off as she did, Dengwi with Venn, Winter safely with Ngarbo. Or did Ustareth only see, watching us all so intently, signs of attachment I missed?)

However, the fact she likes me can't make me hate her, can it. I almost wish—

"Perhaps you'll invite us back," I lamely said.

"Claidi, at any time, any one of you is welcome here. Oh, even Winter, perhaps. But particularly you, you and Argul. I don't think Venn will ever come here again."

She looked—not distressed—just . . . grave.

"That isn't what I want to tell you," she said. "There are three things."

"The magical number in stories."

"Perhaps the *scientific* number. First, I think you'll use your own Power sensibly. When he takes you back among the Hulta"—(she knows; she knows everything always)—"then be very careful. Not that they'll harm you, only they may fear what you can do. What you *are*. Even your Tower-ship is going to trouble them."

I nodded. Argul and I had already discussed making Yin pocket-size, at least to start with. How odd, though, it seems she *didn't* know *that*—

"And also be careful elsewhere, Claidi. There are other scientific marvels scattered about, not mine—old weird and wonderful things that you, and your Power, may wake up as you did the statues in the Grove."

"We saw an *Eye*-gate," I said.

"Yes," she said. "Things like that. Always take care. Although you can protect yourself from any attack, so far my son can't do so through Power alone. And your people can't, either." (She speaks as if I'll be Queen of the Hulta, but the Hulta don't have Queens—their Magician, then. Yes, I'd thought of that already. Being to the Hulta a New Ustareth.)

"Secondly, Claidi, another surprise, I'm afraid. Perhaps unwelcome."

"Which is?"

"You are not a slave, but purely of a royal line."

"*WHAT?*" I jumped up. "But Dengwi—"

She raised her gentle, powerful hand. I sat, and listened.

"Think of what happened at the House," Ustareth said. "The slaves and servants threw down their masters. They let some of the masters stay. Although work there is now shared, at times the masters get much the worst of it. When the sewage needs treating, who do you suppose gets that task? The Free Slaves? No, it will be the fallen princes, like Flindel and

Kerp. Why else did so many of the royalty choose to leave?

"And all this, Claidi, has happened before. Long ago. Even before the time of the Towers. There was a day when all the masters were overthrown in every place, and made into slaves. While the servant-slaves of that time became the princes and princesses. The positions were merely reversed. And from that slave-race-made-master, come the royal Towers, from that slave race come the Princess Ironel, and Jizania, and I come from it, too. Dengwi, whose father is a prince, therefore had for her father a *slave*. Her mother, and yours—the real slave—was of the real and original blood-royal. And so, Claidi, I fear you're truly a princess, since both your parents were slaves. And perhaps you'll become a Queen."

So there I was again, gaping. I, the Powerful Princess, I who would be a Queen.

Is it true? Maybe. Maybe . . .

Oh, well.

"Last of all, the third magical thing I have to tell you."

"Must you?"

She laughed. Then I did, too.

She said, "This third thing you may like. All through this business, they've tried, one way and another, to take away your name. Yes, you were given Winter's intended name, the name of Twilight's daughter—Claidis. But then the name, for you, got changed to Claidi. And *Claidi* is a name in its own right. It comes from an ancient language, ancient as when the Towers were first fighting in the City, a language used for natural things—the land, the animals—and for magic—a language used by those who had psychic Power. Isn't that strange?"

"Yes," I said. What else could I do.

Ustareth said, "The root of the name—look, I'll write it here—is Cla'i'dii. Shall I tell you what it means? *Claaii*, like that, means Wolf, *"i"* means *of* or *on the*, and *"dii"* means Wing. The way the meaning is spoken is just *wolf wing*. And that is your name, Claidi. Wolf on the Wing—Wolf Wing. Does it fit, at all?"

We're going, away and away, over the mountains and the rings of Ustareth's heaven, out over the sea.

In my head, *not* telepathically, I'm still talking to her, to Ustareth the Unforgettable.

I say to her, "But *why* didn't you trust them—the ones you loved? When you were so ill—then more than ever."

And I imagine I hear her say, "I was ashamed of being ill. How could that have happened to *me?* When *I* was the strong one!"

Yes, Ustareth, and you still had to be that strong. Not show a single crack. You thought you were the *only* one strong enough to handle it. And they were all too weak. That's why you didn't give them a chance. That's why you ran away.

And I can't hate you anymore. And—I'm glad I can't.

Venn and Dengwi are in the library here on Yin, making plans. Thu joined them, just possibly because they were eating cake. And no, Venn and Argul have not become best mates. It was too much to hope for. They're very polite to each other, friendly. Trying too hard. Are Dengwi and I still like that? Will *we* get something sorted out. . . . If I'm honest, I'm not sure.

Winter and Ngarbo are now only concerned with each

other. They're down in the room Yinyay formed for them, which makes music. They're dancing. (And a statue appears in case I want to see. I don't and there, it's vanished again. At the moment, I feel, the statues are mostly keeping out of my way.)

Argul's just back from checking on the horses in the stable. He says Yin has added some sort of horse-game to amuse them while we travel—?

Now Argul's sitting across from me, along this gallery. My Argul, to whom I belong. To whom I'll tell everything about these Powers, and ask him, too, if he did find some way to see me on my own journey. But in a while, a little while.

I think—I *know* the Hulta will break their Rule about leaders. I recall what Blurn said, too. They'll make Argul their King all over again, and then, as at the very beginning of all this, he'll be My Argul—Leader of the Hulta.

Only me, then, writing to you, staring out while we soar not too fast over the million-sapphire sea.

And I'm *this* me now. Who I don't know at all, and how do I get used to Her? Perhaps the best, the easiest way, is simply to forget about her (me) most of the time. And remember only, as I fly high up on my wolf wings, to come back again to earth.

CB 1/06

MLib

3/04